U0102232

iHuman
新民说

成
为
更
好
的
人

BOB
DYLAN
THE LYRICS 1961—2012
鲍勃·迪伦诗歌集

地下乡愁蓝调

[美] 鲍勃·迪伦　著

陈黎　张芬龄　胡桑　胡续冬　译

GUANGXI NORMAL UNIVERSITY PRESS
广西师范大学出版社
·桂林·

DIXIA XIANGCHOU LANDIAO

LYRICS: 1961-2012
Copyright © 2016, Bob Dylan
All rights reserved.
著作权合同登记号桂图登字：20-2017-053 号

图书在版编目（CIP）数据

鲍勃·迪伦诗歌集：1961—2012. 地下乡愁蓝调：
汉英对照 /（美）鲍勃·迪伦著；陈黎等译. —桂林：
广西师范大学出版社，2017.6（2018.7 重印）
书名原文：LYRICS：1961-2012
 ISBN 978-7-5495-9690-4

Ⅰ．①鲍…　Ⅱ．①鲍…②陈…　Ⅲ．①诗集－美国－
现代－汉、英　Ⅳ．①I712.25

中国版本图书馆 CIP 数据核字（2017）第 078985 号

出　　版：广西师范大学出版社
　　　　　广西桂林市五里店路 9 号　邮政编码：541004
网　　址：http://www.bbtpress.com
出版人：张艺兵
发　　行：广西师范大学出版社
　　　　　电话：（0773）2802178
印　　刷：山东临沂新华印刷物流集团有限责任公司印刷
　　　　　山东临沂高新技术产业开发区新华路
　　　　　邮政编码：276017
开　　本：740 mm × 1 092 mm　1/32
印　　张：8.25　　　字数：90 千字
版　　次：2017 年 6 月第 1 版　　　2018 年 7 月第 3 次
定　　价：25.00 元

如发现印装质量问题，影响阅读，请与出版社发行部门联系调换

目录

时代正在改变

附加歌词

鲍勃·迪伦的另一面

附加歌词

全数带回家

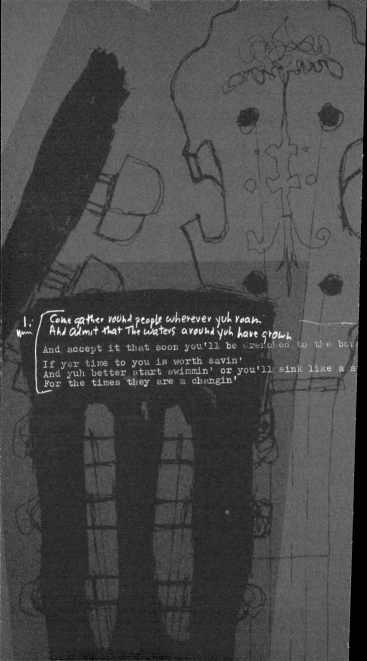

1.

Come gather round people wherever yuh roam
And admit that The waters around yuh have grown
And accept it that soon you'll be drenched to the bone

If yer time to you is worth savin'
And yuh better start swimmin' or you'll sink like a s
For the times they are a changin'

时代正在改变
The Times They Are A-Changin'

陈黎 张芬龄 译

      1964 年 1 月，鲍勃·迪伦发表了他的第三张专辑《时代正在改变》。这张专辑的同名歌曲，敏锐捕捉了正处于十字路口的时代变迁感，呼召新一代的力量和变革精神，既崭新无比，又隐然承续着《旧约·传道书》的源流，成为又一首经典之作。

      一如《时代正在改变》，强烈的现实关怀渗透于此专辑的多首歌曲中。《上帝在我们这一边》反思美国帝国主义与宗教、道德的关系；《北国蓝调》描述明尼苏达州矿产小镇的变迁，为劳动者唱出一阕哀歌；《海蒂·卡罗尔孤独地死去》更融入时事，揭示美国社会种族与阶级之间的矛盾。1963 年 6 月，全国有色人种协进会的重要领袖梅加·埃弗斯（Medgar Evers）在自家门口遭种族隔离分子暗杀，一时舆论哗然。迪伦因而写下《只是棋局里的一枚卒子》，并在同年 8 月马丁·路德·金发表演说的游行集会中献唱。

      除了直面现实之曲，此专辑中也不乏触动人心的柔情之作，如在《西班牙皮靴》《多余的早晨》的旋律中，织入了迪伦与苏西·罗托洛（Suze Rotolo）那段最终无可挽回的恋情。

这张专辑延续上一张的风格，不少歌曲的灵感依然来自传统民谣。使用的乐器仍旧是朴素的口琴和吉他，在巧妙的编排下，却各自得到独特的呈现。譬如经典之作《时代正在改变》，间奏中出现的口琴营造出一种喧哗的氛围，就像 20 世纪 60 年代的空气，陈腐之中，有一股年轻的气息等待被唤起。

编者

时代正在改变 [1]

围聚过来吧，人们

无论你浪迹何方

承认你周遭的

水位已然高涨

并且接受你即将

被浸透的事实

如果你的时间还值得节省

最好开始游泳，否则将像石头一样沉没

因为时代正在改变

来吧，以笔预言的

作家和批评家们

睁大你们的双眼

机会不再登门

话别说得太早

因为轮子 [2] 仍在旋转

---

1. 迪伦在 1985 年精选集《放映机》(*Biograph*) 的说明文字中表示："我想要写一首庞大的歌，短小简洁的段落以一种有催眠效果的方式彼此交叠。民权运动与民谣运动一度非常亲近，在当时联合了。"
2. 轮子，指命运之轮。

无法预知它会指向何人
因为现在的失败者日后将得胜
因为时代正在改变

来吧，参议员和众议员们
请细听这呼吁
不要站在门口
不要堵塞大厅
因为受伤的
将是停滞不前者
外头的战役正如火如荼进行
即将摇撼你的窗子，震响你的墙壁
因为时代正在改变

来吧，全国各地的
母亲和父亲
不要批评你们
不了解的事情
你们的儿女
已不受你们掌控
你们的旧路正迅速老朽
请勿挡住新路，倘若无法伸出援手
因为时代正在改变

界线已划清

诅咒已抛出

现在脚步迟缓者

日后将快速窜出

一如现在这一刻

随后将成为过去

秩序正快速凋落

现在一马当先者日后将居末[1]

因为时代正在改变

1.《新约·马太福音》19:30，耶稣说"然而，有许多在前的，将要在后；在后的，将要在前"。注释凡涉《圣经》处，译文一律引自和合本，供大致的参照。

The Times They Are A-Changin'

Come gather 'round people
Wherever you roam
And admit that the waters
Around you have grown
And accept it that soon
You'll be drenched to the bone
If your time to you is worth savin'
Then you better start swimmin' or you'll sink like a stone
For the times they are a-changin'

Come writers and critics
Who prophesize with your pen
And keep your eyes wide
The chance won't come again
And don't speak too soon
For the wheel's still in spin
And there's no tellin' who that it's namin'
For the loser now will be later to win
For the times they are a-changin'

Come senators, congressmen
Please heed the call
Don't stand in the doorway
Don't block up the hall
For he that gets hurt
Will be he who has stalled
There's a battle outside and it is ragin'
It'll soon shake your windows and rattle your walls
For the times they are a-changin'

Come mothers and fathers
Throughout the land
And don't criticize
What you can't understand
Your sons and your daughters
Are beyond your command
Your old road is rapidly agin'
Please get out of the new one if you can't lend your hand
For the times they are a-changin'

The line it is drawn
The curse it is cast
The slow one now
Will later be fast
As the present now
Will later be past
The order is rapidly fadin'
And the first one now will later be last
For the times they are a-changin'

关于霍利斯·布朗的歌谣

霍利斯·布朗
住在城外某处
霍利斯·布朗
住在城外某处
与老婆和五名子女
以及快塌的小屋

你找工作赚钱
走一英里崎岖路
你找工作赚钱
走一英里崎岖路
你子女如此饥饿
不知微笑为何物

你爱人眼神疯狂
猛拉着你的衣袖
你爱人眼神疯狂
猛拉着你的衣袖
你踱步思索缘由
用尽所有力气

老鼠吃光你家面粉

怨恨找上你家母马

老鼠吃光你家面粉

怨恨找上你家母马

假使有人知道

会有人在乎吗？

你向上帝祈祷

求他送你朋友

你向上帝祈祷

求他送你朋友

口袋空空如你

注定没有朋友

孩子放声大哭

声声重击你脑袋

孩子正放声大哭

声声重击你脑袋

妻子以尖叫戳你

宛如倾盆脏雨

你的绿草变黑

井水已经枯干

你的绿草变黑
井水已经枯干
用最后一美元
你买了七子弹

在远处的荒野
寒冷郊狼嚎叫
在远处的荒野
寒冷郊狼嚎叫
你双眼盯视猎枪
它就挂在墙上

血自你脑中流出
双腿似乎站不住
血自你脑中流出
双腿似乎站不住
你双眼盯视猎枪
它已握在你手上

七阵轻风吹来
绕着屋门打转
七阵轻风吹来
绕着屋门打转

七发子弹作响

有如怒涛拍岸

七个人魂归西天

在南达科他农场

七个人魂归西天

在南达科他农场

遥远的某个地方

七个新人来到世上

Ballad of Hollis Brown

Hollis Brown
He lived on the outside of town
Hollis Brown
He lived on the outside of town
With his wife and five children
And his cabin fallin' down

You looked for work and money
And you walked a rugged mile
You looked for work and money
And you walked a rugged mile
Your children are so hungry
That they don't know how to smile

Your baby's eyes look crazy
They're a-tuggin' at your sleeve
Your baby's eyes look crazy
They're a-tuggin' at your sleeve
You walk the floor and wonder why
With every breath you breathe

The rats have got your flour
Bad blood it got your mare
The rats have got your flour
Bad blood it got your mare
If there's anyone that knows
Is there anyone that cares?

You prayed to the Lord above

Oh please send you a friend
You prayed to the Lord above
Oh please send you a friend
Your empty pockets tell yuh
That you ain't a-got no friend

Your babies are crying louder
It's pounding on your brain
Your babies are crying louder now
It's pounding on your brain
Your wife's screams are stabbin' you
Like the dirty drivin' rain

Your grass it is turning black
There's no water in your well
Your grass is turning black
There's no water in your well
You spent your last lone dollar
On seven shotgun shells

Way out in the wilderness
A cold coyote calls
Way out in the wilderness
A cold coyote calls
Your eyes fix on the shotgun
That's hangin' on the wall

Your brain is a-bleedin'
And your legs can't seem to stand
Your brain is a-bleedin'
And your legs can't seem to stand
Your eyes fix on the shotgun
That you're holdin' in your hand

There's seven breezes a-blowin'
All around the cabin door
There's seven breezes a-blowin'
All around the cabin door
Seven shots ring out
Like the ocean's pounding roar

There's seven people dead
On a South Dakota farm
There's seven people dead
On a South Dakota farm
Somewhere in the distance
There's seven new people born

上帝在我们这一边 [1]

噢，我的姓名不值一提

我的年龄更无意义

我来自的地区

叫作中西部

我在那儿上学长大

遵守法律

我所居住之地

有上帝与它同在

噢，历史课本有说

说得如此清楚

骑兵队进击

印第安人倒下

骑兵队进击

印第安人死去

噢，国家还年轻

上帝从旁提携

---

1. 歌名源自《旧约·诗篇》108:13。

噢，西班牙与美国

曾激战一时 [1]

而内战也是

很快被弭平

英雄的名字

我牢记在心

枪在他们手中

上帝在他们那一边

天啊，第一次世界大战

竟然有终结的一天

开战的原因

我始终未能搞清

但我学会接受

骄傲地接受

因为你不计死亡人数

当上帝在你这一侧

第二次世界大战

结束之后

我们原谅了德国人

---

1. 指 1898 年的美西战争。

变成了朋友

虽然他们杀人六百万

在火化室里受熬煎

德国人现在也

把上帝弄到他们那一边

我学会憎恨俄国人

在我有生之年

另一次大战若开打

我们必须与之一战

恨他们，怕他们

要跑，要躲

也要勇敢接受

上帝在我左右

但如今我们拥有

化学粉尘武器

若是情势所逼

就必须对他们开火

按一下按钮

威力遍及全球

而你从不发问

当上帝在你左右

在许多黑暗时刻

我始终思索此事

耶稣基督

曾被一吻背叛

但我无法代你思考

你得有自己的观点

加略人犹大是否

让上帝站到了他那一边[1]

现在我打算离去

我疲惫不堪

我感到的困惑

没有舌头能言

话语塞满脑中

掉落到地板上

如果上帝在我们这一边

他会拦阻下一次大战

1.《圣经》中，犹大以与耶稣亲嘴为暗号，出卖耶稣。

With God on Our Side

Oh my name it is nothin'
My age it means less
The country I come from
Is called the Midwest
I's taught and brought up there
The laws to abide
And that the land that I live in
Has God on its side

Oh the history books tell it
They tell it so well
The cavalries charged
The Indians fell
The cavalries charged
The Indians died
Oh the country was young
With God on its side

Oh the Spanish-American
War had its day
And the Civil War too
Was soon laid away
And the names of the heroes
I's made to memorize
With guns in their hands
And God on their side

Oh the First World War, boys
It closed out its fate

The reason for fighting
I never got straight
But I learned to accept it
Accept it with pride
For you don't count the dead
When God's on your side

When the Second World War
Came to an end
We forgave the Germans
And we were friends
Though they murdered six million
In the ovens they fried
The Germans now too
Have God on their side

I've learned to hate Russians
All through my whole life
If another war starts
It's them we must fight
To hate them and fear them
To run and to hide
And accept it all bravely
With God on my side

But now we got weapons
Of the chemical dust
If fire them we're forced to
Then fire them we must
One push of the button
And a shot the world wide
And you never ask questions
When God's on your side

Through many dark hour
I've been thinkin' about this
That Jesus Christ
Was betrayed by a kiss
But I can't think for you
You'll have to decide
Whether Judas Iscariot
Had God on his side

So now as I'm leavin'
I'm weary as Hell
The confusion I'm feelin'
Ain't no tongue can tell
The words fill my head
And fall to the floor
If God's on our side
He'll stop the next war

多余的早晨

狗在街道上吠
天色渐渐暗沉
当夜幕低垂
狗吠声渐阑
寂静的夜将会粉碎
被我脑中回荡的喧嚣
因我已是多余的早晨
往事，千里之遥

自门阶前的十字路
我视线开始变暗
当我转头望向我和爱人
曾经躺卧的房间
我回视街道
人行道和路标
而我已是多余的早晨
往事，千里之遥

那是无休止的饥饿感
对任何人都不妙

我述说的每一件事
你可以说得一样妙
你自觉你一切都对
我也自我感觉良好
我俩都是多余的早晨
往事，千里之遥

One Too Many Mornings

Down the street the dogs are barkin'
And the day is a-gettin' dark
As the night comes in a-fallin'
The dogs'll lose their bark
An' the silent night will shatter
From the sounds inside my mind
For I'm one too many mornings
And a thousand miles behind

From the crossroads of my doorstep
My eyes they start to fade
As I turn my head back to the room
Where my love and I have laid
An' I gaze back to the street
The sidewalk and the sign
And I'm one too many mornings
An' a thousand miles behind

It's a restless hungry feeling
That don't mean no one no good
When ev'rything I'm a-sayin'
You can say it just as good
You're right from your side
I'm right from mine
We're both just one too many mornings
An' a thousand miles behind

北国蓝调 [1]

朋友们，围过来
我给你们说个故事
关于那个红色铁矿丰产
而硬纸板遮窗的年代
而长凳上的老人们
跟你说如今整个镇都空了

在小镇的北端
我的孩子们长大成人
但我在另一端成长
在我很小的时候
母亲生病了
我由哥哥带大

当岁月打门口经过
铁矿石源源采出
耙泥机和铲车忙碌不休

---

1. 这首歌中提到的小镇并未说明地名，但令人联想到迪伦的家乡，即美国明
尼苏达州北部的铁矿小镇希宾。

直到有一天我哥

没能回家

一如他之前的我父亲

噢，一个漫漫长冬的等候

我在窗口张望

我的朋友再和善不过

而我的教育中断

因为我在春天辍学

嫁给了约翰·托马斯，一名矿工

噢，岁月再次路过

给的赏赐丰厚

每个季节午餐桶都满溢

随着三个婴儿出生

工作无缘由地

被削减成半天班

不久之后矿井关闭

更多的工作没了

空气中的火似乎冻结了

有个男人前来

他说再过一个星期

第十一号也将关闭

东部的人抱怨
他们出价过高
他们说你们的矿石不值得开采
在南美洲小镇
价格要低廉许多
那里的矿工几乎没拿工钱

因此采矿大门上了锁
任红铁生锈
房里酒味浓重
伤心的无言之歌
使时间加倍漫长
在我等待夕阳西沉的时候

我傍窗而居
他自言自语
舌头的沉默不断堆积
然后有天早上醒来
床上不见人影
他留我只身带着三个小孩

夏天离去

地面寒气日重

店铺接二连三倒闭

我的孩子们也会离去

一旦他们长大

嗯，现在这里没什么留得住他们了

North Country Blues

Come gather 'round friends
And I'll tell you a tale
Of when the red iron pits ran plenty
But the cardboard filled windows
And old men on the benches
Tell you now that the whole town is empty

In the north end of town
My own children are grown
But I was raised on the other
In the wee hours of youth
My mother took sick
And I was brought up by my brother

The iron ore poured
As the years passed the door
The drag lines an' the shovels they was a-humming
'Til one day my brother
Failed to come home
The same as my father before him

Well a long winter's wait
From the window I watched
My friends they couldn't have been kinder
And my schooling was cut
As I quit in the spring
To marry John Thomas, a miner

Oh the years passed again

And the givin' was good
With the lunch bucket filled every season
What with three babies born
The work was cut down
To a half a day's shift with no reason

Then the shaft was soon shut
And more work was cut
And the fire in the air, it felt frozen
'Til a man come to speak
And he said in one week
That number eleven was closin'

They complained in the East
They are paying too high
They say that your ore ain't worth digging
That it's much cheaper down
In the South American towns
Where the miners work almost for nothing

So the mining gates locked
And the red iron rotted
And the room smelled heavy from drinking
Where the sad, silent song
Made the hour twice as long
As I waited for the sun to go sinking

I lived by the window
As he talked to himself
This silence of tongues it was building
Then one morning's wake
The bed it was bare
And I's left alone with three children

The summer is gone
The ground's turning cold
The stores one by one they're a-foldin'
My children will go
As soon as they grow
Well, there ain't nothing here now to hold them

只是棋局里的一枚卒子

灌木丛后方射出的一颗子弹取了梅加·埃弗斯[1]的血

一根手指朝他的名字扣下扳机

一个枪柄藏在暗处

一只手点了火花

两只眼睛瞄准

一个男人的脑后

但不能谴责他

他只是棋局里的一枚卒子

一名南方政客对穷苦白人说教

"你得到的比黑人多，别抱怨

你比他们好命，生下来是白皮肤。"他们解释

假借黑鬼的名义

获取政客的利益

是再清楚不过的道理

他功成名就

---

1. 梅加·埃弗斯（Medgar Evers，1925—1963），美国非裔民权人士，全国有色人种协进会（NAACP）的重要领袖，1963 年 6 月 12 日在家门前下车时遇刺身亡。

而穷苦白人依旧

坐在火车的末车厢

但错不在他

他只是棋局里的一枚卒子

县警察、士兵、州长获得报偿

小镇警察和市警察也都一样

而被玩弄于掌中的穷苦白人宛如工具

从开始上学

他就被灌输此一规则

法律与他同在

为了保护他的白皮肤

维持他的仇恨

所以他从未搞懂

自己所在的处境

但错不在他

他只是棋局里的一枚卒子

出身贫穷棚屋，他自缝隙望向分界线

蹄声在他脑海里咚咚作响

他被教导如何成群结党

自背后开枪

紧握拳头

将人吊死，处以私刑

藏在头巾底下

杀人不觉痛苦

像上了链条的狗

他没有名字

但错不在他

他只是棋局里的一枚卒子

今天，梅加·埃弗斯因中弹而下葬

他像国王般被抬入墓穴

但是当阴暗的阳光落在

开枪那人的身上

他将在自己坟旁看见

留下的墓石上

挨着他的名字

刻着简单的墓志铭：

只是棋局里的一枚卒子

Only a Pawn in Their Game

A bullet from the back of a bush took Medgar Evers' blood
A finger fired the trigger to his name
A handle hid out in the dark
A hand set the spark
Two eyes took the aim
Behind a man's brain
But he can't be blamed
He's only a pawn in their game

A South politician preaches to the poor white man
"You got more than the blacks, don't complain
You're better than them, you been born with white skin,"
    they explain
And the Negro's name
Is used it is plain
For the politician's gain
As he rises to fame
And the poor white remains
On the caboose of the train
But it ain't him to blame
He's only a pawn in their game

The deputy sheriffs, the soldiers, the governors get paid
And the marshals and cops get the same
But the poor white man's used in the hands of them all like
    a tool
He's taught in his school
From the start by the rule
That the laws are with him

To protect his white skin
To keep up his hate
So he never thinks straight
'Bout the shape that he's in
But it ain't him to blame
He's only a pawn in their game

From the poverty shacks, he looks from the cracks to the
    tracks
And the hoofbeats pound in his brain
And he's taught how to walk in a pack
Shoot in the back
With his fist in a clinch
To hang and to lynch
To hide 'neath the hood
To kill with no pain
Like a dog on a chain
He ain't got no name
But it ain't him to blame
He's only a pawn in their game

Today, Medgar Evers was buried from the bullet he caught
They lowered him down as a king
But when the shadowy sun sets on the one
That fired the gun
He'll see by his grave
On the stone that remains
Carved next to his name
His epitaph plain:
Only a pawn in their game

西班牙皮靴

噢，我将扬帆离开我的挚爱
我将在早晨扬帆而去
我可以从我靠岸的地方
跨海寄什么东西给你？

不，并无你可寄之物，我的挚爱
我什么礼物也不期盼
只要你毫发无伤地将自己带回
从寂寞海洋的另一端

噢，我只是想你或许想要某个精品
用金子银子打造的物件
产自马德里山区
或者巴塞罗那海岸

噢，我纵有最暗之夜的明星
纵有最深之海的灿钻
我也会弃之换你甜蜜一吻
唯有那是我心所愿

此次一别也许累月经年

为此我殷殷问

要送你何物让我如在你眼前

让你度日非如年，而如秒如分

噢，你怎可，怎可再问我这问题

徒增我心中伤悲

今日我要你给的同一东西

明日我还会再要一回

寂寥的某日我收到一信

来自她所搭乘的船

她说：我不知道归程是何时辰

要看我心思怎么转

嗯，心爱的，如果你非要那样想

我确定你的心思在游荡

我确定你的心未与我同在

而是在你正前往的异乡

所以要留意，要留意西风

要留意暴风雨的日子

对了，有样东西你可寄回给我

西班牙皮革制的西班牙靴子

Boots of Spanish Leather

Oh, I'm sailin' away my own true love
I'm sailin' away in the morning
Is there something I can send you from across the sea
From the place that I'll be landing?

No, there's nothin' you can send me, my own true love
There's nothin' I wish to be ownin'
Just carry yourself back to me unspoiled
From across that lonesome ocean

Oh, but I just thought you might want something fine
Made of silver or of golden
Either from the mountains of Madrid
Or from the coast of Barcelona

Oh, but if I had the stars from the darkest night
And the diamonds from the deepest ocean
I'd forsake them all for your sweet kiss
For that's all I'm wishin' to be ownin'

That I might be gone a long time
And it's only that I'm askin'
Is there something I can send you to remember me by
To make your time more easy passin'

Oh, how can, how can you ask me again
It only brings me sorrow
The same thing I want from you today
I would want again tomorrow

I got a letter on a lonesome day
It was from her ship a-sailin'
Saying I don't know when I'll be comin' back again
It depends on how I'm a-feelin'

Well, if you, my love, must think that-a-way
I'm sure your mind is roamin'
I'm sure your heart is not with me
But with the country to where you're goin'

So take heed, take heed of the western wind
Take heed of the stormy weather
And yes, there's something you can send back to me
Spanish boots of Spanish leather

大船入港之际 [1]

啊，这样的时候会到来

风将停摆

微风将停止呼吸

仿佛风中的宁静

当飓风仍未兴

在大船入港之际

啊，海面会裂开

大船会到来

海岸线上的沙会抖动

潮声刷刷

风强力吹打

清晨就要破蛹

啊，鱼群会一边大笑

一边游离航道

---

1. 英国传记作家克林顿·黑林（Clinton Heylin）提到，这首歌是迪伦 1963 年 8 月带着怒气在一个旅店房间里写的，此前他邋遢的外表导致店员拒绝他入住，直到琼·贝兹（Joan Baez）担保他品行良好。贝兹在纪录片《没有回家的路》（No Direction Home，2005）中亦提及此事。

海鸥会带着笑意

沙上的岩石

会骄傲地站立

在大船入港之际

所用的语言符号

徒增大船困扰

说出来也无法达意

因为海的链条

会在夜里——断掉

并且深埋于海底

会有歌声欢唱

当主帆变换方向

小船朝向海岸线漂去

太阳会尊敬

甲板上每一张脸孔

在大船入港之际

而后沙子会铺展

一张黄金地毯

让你疲惫的脚趾轻触

大船上的智者

会再次向你提醒，说

整个广阔的世界都在关注！

啊，敌人会起身

眼里睡意仍存

猛然从床上跳起以为还在梦里

但他们掐捏自己，惊声尖叫

确知一切假不了

在大船入港之际

而后他们会高举双手

说：我们会满足你们所有需求

但我们自船首大喊：你们来日可数

一如法老的部众

他们将溺毙于潮水中 [1]

一如歌利亚，他们将被征服 [2]

1.《旧约·出埃及记》14:21-28，耶和华分开红海，摩西引以色列人穿过红海出埃及，埃及人追至半道被复原的海水淹没。

2.《旧约·撒母耳记上》17:48-49，巨人歌利亚被大卫以石头击杀。

When the Ship Comes In

Oh the time will come up
When the winds will stop
And the breeze will cease to be breathin'
Like the stillness in the wind
'Fore the hurricane begins
The hour when the ship comes in

Oh the seas will split
And the ship will hit
And the sands on the shoreline will be shaking
Then the tide will sound
And the wind will pound
And the morning will be breaking

Oh the fishes will laugh
As they swim out of the path
And the seagulls they'll be smiling
And the rocks on the sand
Will proudly stand
The hour that the ship comes in

And the words that are used
For to get the ship confused
Will not be understood as they're spoken
For the chains of the sea
Will have busted in the night
And will be buried at the bottom of the ocean

A song will lift

As the mainsail shifts
And the boat drifts on to the shoreline
And the sun will respect
Every face on the deck
The hour that the ship comes in

Then the sands will roll
Out a carpet of gold
For your weary toes to be a-touchin'
And the ship's wise men
Will remind you once again
That the whole wide world is watchin'

Oh the foes will rise
With the sleep still in their eyes
And they'll jerk from their beds and think they're dreamin'
But they'll pinch themselves and squeal
And know that it's for real
The hour when the ship comes in

Then they'll raise their hands
Sayin' we'll meet all your demands
But we'll shout from the bow your days are numbered
And like Pharoah's tribe
They'll be drownded in the tide
And like Goliath, they'll be conquered

海蒂·卡罗尔孤独地死去 [1]

威廉·赞津格杀死了可怜的海蒂·卡罗尔

用那根他以戴钻戒的手指挥转的手杖

在一家巴尔的摩酒店举行的社交聚会上

警察被找来，拿走他的武器

将他载送到警局拘留

并将威廉·赞津格列为一级谋杀嫌犯

而将耻辱哲学化且批评所有恐惧的你

把帕子从你的脸上拿开

现在还不是流泪的时候

威廉·赞津格，二十四年来

拥有一块占地六百英亩的烟草田

有供养他、保护他的有钱爸妈

以及马里兰州政界的高官亲戚

他对自己行径的回应是耸肩

---

1. 1963 年 2 月 9 日，在美国马里兰州巴尔的摩一家酒店的舞会上，白人威廉·赞津格（William Zantzinger）嫌黑人女招待海蒂·卡罗尔（Hattie Carroll）上酒不够快，辱骂并打伤了她，有心脑血管病史的卡罗尔于八小时后去世。歌词中迪伦将凶手的姓氏 Zantzinger 拼写为 Zanzinger，描述的内容与事实有出入。

咒骂和讥讽，他的舌头不停叫嚣
过了几分钟，他获保释走了出去
而将耻辱哲学化且批评所有恐惧的你
把帕子从你的脸上拿开
现在还不是流泪的时候

海蒂·卡罗尔是厨房的女佣
她五十一岁，生了十个小孩
她端盘子，倒垃圾
从未坐上餐桌的一端
甚至不曾跟用餐的人说话
她只是将餐桌的食物收拾干净
清空另一楼层的烟灰缸
却被一记重击杀害，被一根手杖击毙
手杖腾空飞越，穿过房间落下
命中注定要摧毁这位温和妇人
她从未对威廉·赞津格做过任何事
而将耻辱哲学化且批评所有恐惧的你
把帕子从你的脸上拿开
现在还不是流泪的时候

在崇高的法庭上，法官重重敲击小木槌
表示人人平等而且法院公平正直

已结之案是不容操纵或说动的

即便贵族也会受到应得的处置

一旦被警察追捕到案

法律之梯无顶也无底

盯视着这名犯人，他杀人没有缘由

恰好心血来潮，没有预警

法官说话了，透过极有深度又高雅的法袍

强有力地作出，为了惩罚和使其悔改

威廉·赞津格刑期六个月的判决

噢，而将耻辱哲学化且批评所有恐惧的你

把帕子深深埋进脸里

因为现在是该流泪的时候了

The Lonesome Death of Hattie Carroll

William Zanzinger killed poor Hattie Carroll
With a cane that he twirled around his diamond ring finger
At a Baltimore hotel society gath'rin'
And the cops were called in and his weapon took from him
As they rode him in custody down to the station
And booked William Zanzinger for first-degree murder
But you who philosophize disgrace and criticize all fears
Take the rag away from your face
Now ain't the time for your tears

William Zanzinger, who at twenty-four years
Owns a tobacco farm of six hundred acres
With rich wealthy parents who provide and protect him
And high office relations in the politics of Maryland
Reacted to his deed with a shrug of his shoulders
And swear words and sneering, and his tongue it was
    snarling
In a matter of minutes on bail was out walking
But you who philosophize disgrace and criticize all fears
Take the rag away from your face
Now ain't the time for your tears

Hattie Carroll was a maid of the kitchen
She was fifty-one years old and gave birth to ten children
Who carried the dishes and took out the garbage
And never sat once at the head of the table
And didn't even talk to the people at the table
Who just cleaned up all the food from the table
And emptied the ashtrays on a whole other level

Got killed by a blow, lay slain by a cane
That sailed through the air and came down through the room
Doomed and determined to destroy all the gentle
And she never done nothing to William Zanzinger
But you who philosophize disgrace and criticize all fears
Take the rag away from your face
Now ain't the time for your tears

In the courtroom of honor, the judge pounded his gavel
To show that all's equal and that the courts are on the level
And that the strings in the books ain't pulled and persuaded
And that even the nobles get properly handled
Once that the cops have chased after and caught 'em
And that the ladder of law has no top and no bottom
Stared at the person who killed for no reason
Who just happened to be feelin' that way without warnin'
And he spoke through his cloak, most deep and distinguished
And handed out strongly, for penalty and repentance
William Zanzinger with a six-month sentence
Oh, but you who philosophize disgrace and criticize all fears
Bury the rag deep in your face
For now's the time for your tears

无休止的道别 [1]

噢，我此生所花之钱

不管得之有道或来路不当

我乐于让它溜过我朋友之手

用力将时间系住

但酒瓶空了

我们喝光了每一瓶酒

餐桌满到要溢出

而角落的告示牌

写着要打烊了

所以我将道别，上路

噢，我抚摸过的每个女孩

我并非出于恶意

而我伤害过的每个女孩

我并非刻意为之

但若要继续当朋友

弥补过失

1.《新闻周刊》(*Newsweek*) 在 1963 年刊文指责迪伦捏造出身等个人信息，
这首歌对此有所回应。

你需要时间继续逗留

而如今我双脚急着

与过去背道而驰

我将道别，沿着街道前行

噢，我遇过的每个对手

我们来到之前目标已定

而我奋斗过的每个目标

我全力以赴，无悔无愧

但黑暗当真会消失

当窗帘被拉起，某个人的眼睛

就必须迎向黎明

如果看到白昼

我就只好伫留

所以我将在夜晚道别，离去

噢，在我脑海打结的每个思绪

如果跳不出，我可能会疯掉

但我不要光溜溜地站在陌生人面前

我要为自己和朋友唱出我的故事

但时间不多，而你只能仰仗时间

没有话语会独留哪位特殊朋友心头

虽然断了线

但还不到尽头

我将只是道别，后会有期

噢，虚假的时钟想滴答掉我的时间

以玷污我、分散我心思、烦扰我

流言蜚语的污垢吹到我脸上

谣言的尘埃覆盖我身上

但如果箭是直的

箭头够利落

再厚的灰尘它也可射穿

所以我会坚定立场

保持本色

然后道别，毫不在乎

Restless Farewell

Oh all the money that in my whole life I did spend
Be it mine right or wrongfully
I let it slip gladly past the hands of my friends
To tie up the time most forcefully
But the bottles are done
We've killed each one
And the table's full and overflowed
And the corner sign
Says it's closing time
So I'll bid farewell and be down the road

Oh ev'ry girl that ever I've touched
I did not do it harmfully
And ev'ry girl that ever I've hurt
I did not do it knowin'ly
But to remain as friends
And make amends
You need the time and stay behind
And since my feet are now fast
And point away from the past
I'll bid farewell and be down the line

Oh ev'ry foe that ever I faced
The cause was there before we came
And ev'ry cause that ever I fought
I fought it full without regret or shame
But the dark does die
As the curtain is drawn and somebody's eyes
Must meet the dawn

And if I see the day
I'd only have to stay
So I'll bid farewell in the night and be gone

Oh, ev'ry thought that's strung a knot in my mind
I might go insane if it couldn't be sprung
But it's not to stand naked under unknowin' eyes
It's for myself and my friends my stories are sung
But the time ain't tall, yet on time you depend
And no word is possessed by no special friend
And though the line is cut
It ain't quite the end
I'll just bid farewell till we meet again

Oh a false clock tries to tick out my time
To disgrace, distract, and bother me
And the dirt of gossip blows into my face
And the dust of rumors covers me
But if the arrow is straight
And the point is slick
It can pierce through dust no matter how thick
So I'll make my stand
And remain as I am
And bid farewell and not give a damn

永恒的圆

我缓缓唱出那首歌时
她站在阴暗处
她移步光中时
我拨动银色琴弦
她用眼睛召唤
与我弹奏的旋律应和
但那首歌很长
而我才刚开始唱

透过射出的灯光
她的脸回应着
自我舌尖滚动出的
快速流逝的歌词
远远看去
她的眼睛火光四射
但那首歌很长
有更多还没唱

我的目光舞出一个圆
圈住她清晰的身形

她把头侧向一边

再次向我召唤

当旋律飘出

回声里她呼吸急促

但那首歌很长

还要很久才能唱完

我瞧了瞧吉他

弹奏着，假装

台下所有的眼睛

我压根没看到

而她的心思重重袭来

仿佛箭矢刺入

但那首歌很长

必须把它唱完

曲子总算告终

我放下吉他

寻找那个刚才

待了很久的女孩

我寻寻觅觅

不见伊人身影

只好拿起吉他

开始下一首歌

Eternal Circle

I sang the song slowly
As she stood in the shadows
She stepped to the light
As my silver strings spun
She called with her eyes
To the tune I's a-playin'
But the song it was long
And I'd only begun

Through a bullet of light
Her face was reflectin'
The fast fading words
That rolled from my tongue
With a long-distance look
Her eyes was on fire
But the song it was long
And there was more to be sung

My eyes danced a circle
Across her clear outline
With her head tilted sideways
She called me again
As the tune drifted out
She breathed hard through the echo
But the song it was long
And it was far to the end

I glanced at my guitar
And played it pretendin'

That of all the eyes out there
I could see none
As her thoughts pounded hard
Like the pierce of an arrow
But the song it was long
And it had to get done

As the tune finally folded
I laid down the guitar
Then looked for the girl
Who'd stayed for so long
But her shadow was missin'
For all of my searchin'
So I picked up my guitar
And began the next song

胜利之道

纷扰之径
战役之路
胜利之道
我将踏上

小径尘扬
路或崎岖
顺境在望
不远矣，二三子！

纷扰之径
战役之路
胜利之道
吾人将踏上

我沿河而行
我高仰我头
我见银线 [1]

---

1. 指云朵的银色边缘，喻一线希望。

悬于天际

纷扰之径
战役之路
胜利之道
吾人将踏上

暮色翻卷
我行于小径
有风吹拂
吹拂我背

纷扰之径
战役之路
胜利之道
吾人将踏上

碎石路崎岖
路阻难行
宽途在望
煤渣两边铺

纷扰之径

战役之路

胜利之道

吾人将踏上

夜车滚滚前进

车轮一路哼唱

眼见更佳之日

在原野彼方

纷扰之径

战役之路

胜利之道

吾人将踏上

小径尘扬

路或崎岖

顺境在望

不远矣，二三子！

纷扰之径

战役之路

胜利之道

吾人将踏上

Paths of Victory

Trails of troubles
Roads of battles
Paths of victory
I shall walk

The trail is dusty
And my road it might be rough
But the better roads are waiting
And boys it ain't far off

Trails of troubles
Roads of battles
Paths of victory
We shall walk

I walked down by the river
I turned my head up high
I saw that silver linin'
That was hangin' in the sky

Trails of troubles
Roads of battles
Paths of victory
We shall walk

The evenin' dusk was rollin'
I was walking down the track
There was a one-way wind a-blowin'
And it was blowin' at my back

Trails of troubles
Roads of battles
Paths of victory
We shall walk

The gravel road is bumpy
It's a hard road to ride
But there's a clearer road a-waitin'
With the cinders on the side

Trails of troubles
Roads of battles
Paths of victory
We shall walk

That evening train was rollin'
The hummin' of its wheels
My eyes they saw a better day
As I looked across the fields

Trails of troubles
Roads of battles
Paths of victory
We shall walk

The trail is dusty
The road it might be rough
But the good road is a-waitin'
And boys it ain't far off

Trails of troubles
Roads of battles

Paths of victory
We shall walk

只不过一个流浪汉

有一天我外出走过街角
看到一个老流浪汉，躺在门口
整张脸紧贴在人行道冰冷的地面上
我想他在那儿已待了整晚或者更长

只不过一个流浪汉，但又一个流浪汉走了
没有人留下为他唱哀歌
没有人留下抬他回家
只不过一个流浪汉，但又一个流浪汉走了

报纸做成的毯子盖住他的头颅
路缘石是他的枕头，马路是他的床铺
看一眼他的脸可知他一路走来的艰辛
一拳头的硬币是他乞讨得来的钱

只不过一个流浪汉，但又一个流浪汉走了
没有人留下为他唱哀歌
没有人留下抬他回家
只不过一个流浪汉，但又一个流浪汉走了

一个人看到自己的一生走下坡是否心痛难挨

从地洞抬头看世界

像瘸马一般等候未来

躺在排水沟，无名无姓地离开？

只不过一个流浪汉，但又一个流浪汉走了

没有人留下为他唱哀歌

没有人留下抬他回家

只不过一个流浪汉，但又一个流浪汉走了

Only a Hobo

As I was out walking on a corner one day
I spied an old hobo, in a doorway he lay
His face was all grounded in the cold sidewalk floor
And I guess he'd been there for the whole night or more

Only a hobo, but one more is gone
Leavin' nobody to sing his sad song
Leavin' nobody to carry him home
Only a hobo, but one more is gone

A blanket of newspaper covered his head
As the curb was his pillow, the street was his bed
One look at his face showed the hard road he'd come
And a fistful of coins showed the money he bummed

Only a hobo, but one more is gone
Leavin' nobody to sing his sad song
Leavin' nobody to carry him home
Only a hobo, but one more is gone

Does it take much of a man to see his whole life go down
To look up on the world from a hole in the ground
To wait for your future like a horse that's gone lame
To lie in the gutter and die with no name?

Only a hobo, but one more is gone
Leavin' nobody to sing his sad song
Leavin' nobody to carry him home
Only a hobo, but one more is gone

歇下你疲惫的曲调 [1]

歇下你疲惫的曲调，歇下
歇下你的歌，不再随兴拨弹
让自己在琴弦的力量下休憩
任何声音都不许哼唱

被日出前的声音触动
我知道夜已消失无形
晨风如号角般吹着
与黎明的鼓声唱应

歇下你疲惫的曲调，歇下
歇下你的歌，不再随兴拨弹
让自己在琴弦的力量下休憩
任何声音都不许哼唱

汹涌的海如管风琴般演奏

---

1. 迪伦在 1985 年精选集《放映机》的说明文字中表示："我是在西海岸琼·贝兹的房子里写（这首歌）的……我从一张 78 转的黑胶老唱片上听到一首苏格兰民谣，我尝试真正地捕捉到那种萦绕着我的感觉。"

海草编织着它的绳线
拍岸的碎浪像钹一般
与岩块和沙砾互相击撞

歇下你疲惫的曲调，歇下
歇下你的歌，不再随兴拨弹
让自己在琴弦的力量下休憩
任何声音都不许哼唱

我悠哉站着，头上的天空
和云朵远离一切法律的镣铐
哭泣的雨歌唱如小号
不求掌声回报

歇下你疲惫的曲调，歇下
歇下你的歌，不再随兴拨弹
让自己在琴弦的力量下休憩
任何声音都不许哼唱

最后的叶片自树上掉落
依偎于新恋人的怀中
秃枝弹奏如班卓琴
风是最佳的听众

我低头凝视河水镜面
见它迂回曲折自由弹
光洁河水流动如圣歌
仿佛竖琴哼唱

歇下你疲惫的曲调，歇下
歇下你的歌，不再随兴拨弹
让自己在琴弦的力量下休憩
任何声音都不许哼唱

Lay Down Your Weary Tune

Lay down your weary tune, lay down
Lay down the song you strum
And rest yourself 'neath the strength of strings
No voice can hope to hum

Struck by the sounds before the sun
I knew the night had gone
The morning breeze like a bugle blew
Against the drums of dawn

Lay down your weary tune, lay down
Lay down the song you strum
And rest yourself 'neath the strength of strings
No voice can hope to hum

The ocean wild like an organ played
The seaweed's wove its strands
The crashin' waves like cymbals clashed
Against the rocks and sands

Lay down your weary tune, lay down
Lay down the song you strum
And rest yourself 'neath the strength of strings
No voice can hope to hum

I stood unwound beneath the skies
And clouds unbound by laws
The cryin' rain like a trumpet sang
And asked for no applause

Lay down your weary tune, lay down
Lay down the song you strum
And rest yourself 'neath the strength of strings
No voice can hope to hum

The last of leaves fell from the trees
And clung to a new love's breast
The branches bare like a banjo played
To the winds that listened best

I gazed down in the river's mirror
And watched its winding strum
The water smooth ran like a hymn
And like a harp did hum

Lay down your weary tune, lay down
Lay down the song you strum
And rest yourself 'neath the strength of strings
No voice can hope to hum

珀西之歌

坏消息，坏消息
传到我睡觉的地方
翻转，翻转，再翻转
说你的一个朋友
惹上大麻烦
翻转，翻转成雨
成风

告诉我是何麻烦
对着我耳朵说一遍
翻转，翻转，再翻转
乔利埃特监狱
而且九十九年
翻转，翻转成雨
成风

噢，罪名为何
怎么会这样
翻转，翻转，再翻转
杀人致死

一级重罪

翻转，翻转成雨

成风

我坐下来尽全力

写出最好的文字

翻转，翻转，再翻转

向法官说明

我星期三晚上会到

翻转，翻转成雨

成风

未获回信

我在月色中出发

翻转，翻转，再翻转

第二天下午

到了他的办公室

翻转，翻转成雨

成风

你可否告知实情？

我无所惧地说

翻转，翻转，再翻转

我的一位朋友
被判九十九年
翻转，翻转成雨
成风

公路上的一次车祸
让一辆车飞进田里
翻转，翻转，再翻转
有四个人死亡
而他是驾驶者
翻转，翻转成雨
成风

但我了解他
就像了解我自己
翻转，翻转，再翻转
他不会伤害
他人的性命
翻转，翻转成雨
成风

法官开口
刻意压低声音

翻转，翻转，再翻转

说："目击者对此

几乎毫无疑问"

翻转，翻转成雨

成风

或许的确如此

他得入监服刑

翻转，翻转，再翻转

但九十九年

不是他应得的

翻转，翻转成雨

成风

太迟了，太迟了

因为他的案子已结

翻转，翻转，再翻转

他的刑期已定

不可能撤销

翻转，翻转成雨

成风

但他并非罪犯

未犯什么罪

翻转，翻转，再翻转

发生在他身上的事

任何人都可能碰上

翻转，翻转成雨

成风

此时法官突然向前一凑

一脸僵冷

翻转，翻转，再翻转

说："可否行行好，请现在

离开我的办公室"

翻转，翻转成雨

成风

嗯，他的眼神显得滑稽

我很慢很慢地起身

翻转，翻转，再翻转

除了离开

别无选择

翻转，翻转成雨

成风

我走到走廊

听到门砰然关上

翻转，翻转，再翻转

我走下法庭的台阶

无法理解

翻转，翻转成雨

成风

我弹奏吉他

从晚上弹到天明

翻转，翻转，再翻转

而我的吉他所能

弹出的唯一曲调

是："噢，残忍的雨

及风"

Percy's Song

Bad news, bad news
Come to me where I sleep
Turn, turn, turn again
Sayin' one of your friends
Is in trouble deep
Turn, turn to the rain
And the wind

Tell me the trouble
Tell once to my ear
Turn, turn, turn again
Joliet prison
And ninety-nine years
Turn, turn to the rain
And the wind

Oh what's the charge
Of how this came to be
Turn, turn, turn again
Manslaughter
In the highest of degree
Turn, turn to the rain
And the wind

I sat down and wrote
The best words I could write
Turn, turn, turn again
Explaining to the judge
I'd be there on Wednesday night

Turn, turn to the rain
And the wind

Without a reply
I left by the moon
Turn, turn, turn again
And was in his chambers
By the next afternoon
Turn, turn to the rain
And the wind

Could ya tell me the facts?
I said without fear
Turn, turn, turn again
That a friend of mine
Would get ninety-nine years
Turn, turn to the rain
And the wind

A crash on the highway
Flew the car to a field
Turn, turn, turn again
There was four persons killed
And he was at the wheel
Turn, turn to the rain
And the wind

But I knew him as good
As I'm knowin' myself
Turn, turn, turn again
And he wouldn't harm a life
That belonged to someone else
Turn, turn to the rain

And the wind

The judge spoke
Out of the side of his mouth
Turn, turn, turn again
Sayin', "The witness who saw
He left little doubt"
Turn, turn to the rain
And the wind

That may be true
He's got a sentence to serve
Turn, turn, turn again
But ninety-nine years
He just don't deserve
Turn, turn to the rain
And the wind

Too late, too late
For his case it is sealed
Turn, turn, turn again
His sentence is passed
And it cannot be repealed
Turn, turn to the rain
And the wind

But he ain't no criminal
And his crime it is none
Turn, turn, turn again
What happened to him
Could happen to anyone
Turn, turn to the rain
And the wind

And at that the judge jerked forward
And his face it did freeze
Turn, turn, turn again
Sayin', "Could you kindly leave
My office now, please"
Turn, turn to the rain
And the wind

Well his eyes looked funny
And I stood up so slow
Turn, turn, turn again
With no other choice
Except for to go
Turn, turn to the rain
And the wind

I walked down the hallway
And I heard his door slam
Turn, turn, turn again
I walked down the courthouse stairs
And I did not understand
Turn, turn to the rain
And the wind

And I played my guitar
Through the night to the day
Turn, turn, turn again
And the only tune
My guitar could play
Was, "Oh the Cruel Rain
And the Wind"

我想我过得不错

嗯，我没有了童年
或我曾认识的朋友
是的，我没有了童年
或我曾认识的朋友
但我还留着我的声音
可以带着它四处走
嘿嘿，所以我想我过得不错

我不曾有过很多钱
但总还能设法露露脸
是的，我不曾有过很多钱
但总还能设法露露脸
我曾多次弯腰
但尚未低过头
嘿嘿，所以我想我过得不错

烦忧啊，烦忧
烦忧在我心头
烦忧啊，烦忧
烦忧在我心头

但世上的烦忧，主啊

比我的大得多

嘿嘿，所以我想我过得不错

我不曾坐拥军队

听我命令东奔西走

是的，我不曾坐拥军队

听我命令东奔西走

但我不需要军队

我有一个好友

嘿嘿，所以我想我过得不错

我曾被踢、被鞭打、被践踏

曾遭到枪击，与你相同

我曾被踢、被鞭打、被践踏

曾遭到枪击，与你相同。

但只要世界持续转动

我也会持续转动

嘿嘿，所以我想我过得不错

嗯，我的路上或许满布岩块

石头或许会划伤我的脸

我的路上或许满布岩块

石头或许会划伤我的脸

但有些人却完全无路可走

只能一直站在原点

嘿嘿，所以我想我过得不错

Guess I'm Doin' Fine

Well, I ain't got my childhood
Or friends I once did know
No, I ain't got my childhood
Or friends I once did know
But I still got my voice left
I can take it anywhere I go
Hey, hey, so I guess I'm doin' fine

And I've never had much money
But I'm still around somehow
No, I've never had much money
But I'm still around somehow
Many times I've bended
But I ain't never yet bowed
Hey, hey, so I guess I'm doin' fine

Trouble, oh trouble
I've trouble on my mind
Trouble, oh trouble
Trouble on my mind
But the trouble in the world, Lord
Is much more bigger than mine
Hey, hey, so I guess I'm doin' fine

And I never had no armies
To jump at my command
No, I ain't got no armies
To jump at my command
But I don't need no armies

I got me one good friend
Hey, hey, so I guess I'm doin' fine

I been kicked and whipped and trampled on
I been shot at just like you
I been kicked and whipped and trampled on
I been shot at just like you.
But as long as the world keeps a-turnin'
I just keep a-turnin' too
Hey, hey, so I guess I'm doin' fine

Well, my road might be rocky
The stones might cut my face
My road it might be rocky
The stones might cut my face
But as some folks ain't got no road at all
They gotta stand in the same old place
Hey, hey, so I guess I'm doin' fine

Some other kinds of songs…

Poems by Bob Dylan

baby black's
been had
aint bad
snickerstacked
chicken shacked
dressed in black
silver monkey
on her back
mammy ma
juiced pa
janitored
between the law
brother's ton
rat-faced
gravestoned
ditch dug
firesceped an subsroked
choked
baby black
hits back
robs, pawns
lives by trade
sits an waits on fire plug
digs the heat
eyes meet
picket line
across the street
head rings
of bed springs
freedom's holler
you askd order
she'd knock
the world
for a dollar an a quarter
baby black
dressed in
gunny sack
about t crack
been gone
carry on
i'm givin you
myself t pawn

for françoise hardy
at the seine's edge
a giant shadow
of notre dame
seeks t grab my foot
sorbonne students
whirl by on thin blue
swirlin lifelike colors of leather spin
the breeze yawns food
far from the bells
of erhardt meet
piles of lovers
fishing
kissing
lay themselves on
old men
clothed in curly mustaches
float on the benches
blankets of tourists
in bright red velour shirts
with straw hats of ambassadors
(cannot hear sinatra's
dawg bark now)
will sail away
as the sun goes down
the doors of the river are open
i must remember that
i too play the guitar
it's easy t stand here
more lovers pass
on motorcycles
roped together
from the walls of the water then
i look across t what they call
the right bank
an envy
your
trumpet
player

"i could make you crawl"

"what d you mean?"
"i mean i lose all the time"
his jaw tightened an he look
a deep breath
"hummm, now i gotta beat you!"

straight away an into the ring
juno takes twenty pills an
paints all day, life he says
is a head kinda thing, outside
of chicago, private coma down
junkie nurse home heals countless
common housewives strung out
fully on drugstore dope, legally
sold t help clean the kitchen
lenny bruce shows his seventh
avenue hand made movies, while a
bunch of women sneak little white
tablets into shoes, stockings, hats
an other hidin places, newspapers
fall neither, irma goes t israel
an writes me that there, they
hate nazis much more n we over here
do, eichmann dies yes, an west
germany sends eighty year old
pruned out gestapo hermit off t
the penitentary, at jest be in
tie t get in t this certain place
i wanna go back here, literate
old man with rubel flag above
home sweet home sign says he wont
go no further, "talks too
much" the mad hatter, an see
that little boy who lives on see
saw street, an man in the get
that little boy who "mediated"
buy miller t sends on other side
of ping pong table an keeps
talkin about me, "did you ask
the poet fellow if he wants
something t drink" he says t
someone gettin all the drinks
i don't my ping pong paddle
an look at the poet, my worst
friend, you put me down but
you are a mysterious way
i'm crashin on the machine
an trophies on the wall
he rattles off names an mumbles
he then answers my question, he
says, "no, i dont
gets all squishy, i say
answer the next question
your question, ferris wheel turns
in california an the sky trembles
turns red, the seeds weed
astronomical books an old
i break my ask with wuld
wants mo t say wha she
can understand, t force tempered fat
man in borrowed stomach slam wife
in the face an rushes off t civil
rights meeting, while some strange
girl chases me up smoky mountain
tryin t find out what sign i am,
i take alan ginsberg t meet fantastic
great beautiful artist an do trespassin

boards block up all there is t see
eviction, infection gangrene an
atom bombs, both ends exist only
because there is someone who wants
profit, boy loses eyesight, becomes
airplane pilot, people pound their
chests an other people's chests an
interpret bibles t suit their own
means, respect is just a misinterpreted word
an if jesus christ, himself, came
down thru these streets, Christianity
would start all over again, standin

between pillars of chips
springs up from the cushion
thumps thumps
strikes
is on the prowl
you'll only lose
shouldnt stay
jack o' diamonds
is a hard t play

jack o' diamonds
wrecked my hand
left me here t stand
little tin men play
their drums now
upside my head
in the midst of cheers
flowers
four queens
with pawed out hearts
make make believe
they're stuff good
but i should drop
fold
an dean martin should apologize
t the rolling stone
ho hum
young actors
their fathers' necks
two dudes in hopped up ford
for the tenth time
have rolled thru town
its your turn baby t
set the deck
oh you're goin under
stayed too long
chinese colors
jack o' diamonds
(but ain't high enough)

jack o' diamonds
is a hard card t play

jack o' diamonds used t laugh at me
now wants t collect from me
used t be ashamed of me
now wants t walk long side of me
jack o' diamonds
one armed prince
wears but a single glove
as he shaves
an as he's fixed mirrors
roved t room at nite
there's somethin
in my drink
would plow it in his face
but it'd do no good
gin no good
jack o' diamonds

as he gets old
his hair neonddrop bag
no more ashtrays
can t even remember
the early days
please dont stay
gather your bells an go
jack o' diamonds
(can open for riches)
jack o' diamonds
(but then it switches)
a colorful picture but
beats only the ten
jack o' diamonds
is a hard card t play

jack o' diamonds stays indoors
wants me t fight his wars
jack o' diamonds is a hard card t
never certain, in the middle
commentin on the songs of birds
chucklin at screamin mothers
jack o' diamonds drains
fish brains
rattles what's left over

Handwritten overlay:

It aint me babe it aint me you're looking for

Oh you say that you are looking
for someone who is strong
~~t protect t~~ protect you ~~from all~~ sadness
An defend you right or wrong
but

Oh you say
you say that
oh ~~you say that~~ you are looking
~~for t~~ for a ~~true~~ heart t be so true
~~some one~~ you can count on hot t leave
An t love nothing else but you

your ~~red~~ eyes ~~They run~~ ~~tell your~~ fortune
your words ~~run~~
~~your whispering~~ like water they flowin
~~but~~ ~~t tell you wishes~~
but I'm afraid I cant + the go...

鲍勃·迪伦的另一面
Another Side of Bob Dylan

胡桑 译

　　第四张专辑《鲍勃·迪伦的另一面》，在 1964 年 8 月 8 日由哥伦比亚唱片公司发行。从商业角度来看，这张专辑并不算成功，只位列《公告牌》专辑榜第四十三名，但在一定程度上，这可以说是鲍勃·迪伦承上启下之作。

　　在编曲制作上，除常用的木吉他和口琴外，《黑鸦蓝调》一曲还首次使用了钢琴。就歌词而言，在这张专辑中，迪伦弱化了社会意识，不再着重于针砭时弊。虽然《自由的钟乐》一曲依旧延续了之前的主题，但与前作相比，总体上减少了反抗性和批判性。他把视野由社会宏观领域更多地投至私人化的情感世界，如《朴素 D 调歌谣》直白地描述了与前女友苏西分手的场景，又如《西班牙哈莱姆事件》流露出对吉普赛女人的爱慕，以及对流浪生活的无限神往。尽管迪伦当时正处于分手后的低谷，他却自我解嘲，将滑稽的亨德尔唱法运用到情歌的演绎之中，并不时对庸俗的爱情套路加以调侃，譬如《我真正想做的一切》

《那不是我，宝贝》等作品。受到兰波等象征派诗人的影响，迪伦还在《我的往昔岁月》等歌曲中运用了含混朦胧的隐喻。透过这些歌词，确如专辑名字，可以窥见迪伦的另外一面。

胡桑

我真正想做的一切

我并不希望与你竞争
对你施打，欺骗，或虐待
将你简化，将你分类
对你拒绝、蔑视或折磨
我真正想做的一切
就是，宝贝，与你成为朋友

不，我并不希望与你打斗
让你恐惧，或让你紧张
拖垮你，或耗尽你
绑缚你，或击败你
我真正想做的一切
就是，宝贝，与你成为朋友

我并不希望妨碍你
把你惊扰，搞大，或锁住
将你分析，将你归类
将你确定，或将你宣传
我真正想做的一切
就是，宝贝，与你成为朋友

我不想直接面对你

与你赛跑或追逐，对你跟踪或尾随

或羞辱你，或取代你

或定义你，或限制你

我真正想做的一切

就是，宝贝，与你成为朋友

我不想见到你的亲戚

让你晕眩，或搞垮你

或选择你，或剖析你

或检查你，或拒绝你

我真正想做的一切

就是，宝贝，与你成为朋友

我不想捉弄你

除掉你，抖落你或抛弃你

我不希求你像我那样感觉

像我那样理解或变得像我一样

我真正想做的一切

就是，宝贝，与你成为朋友

All I Really Want to Do

I ain't lookin' to compete with you
Beat or cheat or mistreat you
Simplify you, classify you
Deny, defy or crucify you
All I really want to do
Is, baby, be friends with you

No, and I ain't lookin' to fight with you
Frighten you or tighten you
Drag you down or drain you down
Chain you down or bring you down
All I really want to do
Is, baby, be friends with you

I ain't lookin' to block you up
Shock or knock or lock you up
Analyze you, categorize you
Finalize you or advertise you
All I really want to do
Is, baby, be friends with you

I don't want to straight-face you
Race or chase you, track or trace you
Or disgrace you or displace you
Or define you or confine you
All I really want to do
Is, baby, be friends with you

I don't want to meet your kin

Make you spin or do you in
Or select you or dissect you
Or inspect you or reject you
All I really want to do
Is, baby, be friends with you

I don't want to fake you out
Take or shake or forsake you out
I ain't lookin' for you to feel like me
See like me or be like me
All I really want to do
Is, baby, be friends with you

黑鸦蓝调

我在清晨醒来，游荡
憔悴又疲惫
我在清晨醒来，游荡
憔悴又疲惫
希望我久违的恋人
会来到我面前，和我说话
告诉我这一切是怎么回事

我站立在侧边小路
听着广告牌砰砰作响
站立在侧边小路
听着广告牌砰砰作响
嗯，我的手腕空空
但我的神经在跳动
就像时钟走着

如果我有什么是你需要的，宝贝
让我说在前头
如果我有什么是你需要的，宝贝
让我说在前头

你可以在某个时候来找我

夜晚也好，白天也行

就看你什么时候想来

有时我在想我

太高而无法下落

有时我在想我

太高而无法下落

别的时候我在想我

是那么低，我不知道

自己到底能否上来

草原上的黑乌鸦

越过一条宽阔的公路

草原上的黑乌鸦

越过一条宽阔的公路

虽然这很可笑，亲爱的

我今天只是不太觉得

自己像一个稻草人

Black Crow Blues

I woke in the mornin', wand'rin'
Wasted and worn out
I woke in the mornin', wand'rin'
Wasted and worn out
Wishin' my long-lost lover
Will walk to me, talk to me
Tell me what it's all about

I was standin' at the side road
Listenin' to the billboard knock
Standin' at the side road
Listenin' to the billboard knock
Well, my wrist was empty
But my nerves were kickin'
Tickin' like a clock

If I got anything you need, babe
Let me tell you in front
If I got anything you need, babe
Let me tell you in front
You can come to me sometime
Night time, day time
Any time you want

Sometimes I'm thinkin' I'm
Too high to fall
Sometimes I'm thinkin' I'm
Too high to fall
Other times I'm thinkin' I'm

So low I don't know
If I can come up at all

Black crows in the meadow
Across a broad highway
Black crows in the meadow
Across a broad highway
Though it's funny, honey
I just don't feel much like a
Scarecrow today

西班牙哈莱姆[1]事件

吉普赛姑娘，哈莱姆的手

其热度无法留住你

你的身体太烫，难以平抑

你燃烧的双足焚毁了街道

我无家可归，来让我

感受到你咚咚响的鼓

让我知道，宝贝，知道我的命运

顺着我不安的掌纹

吉普赛姑娘，你吞下了我

我已深深沦陷

你珍珠般的双眸，如此灵活而明洁

你的牙齿闪烁如钻石

夜晚黑如沥青，来让我

苍白的脸适于此地，啊，行行好吧！

让我知道，宝贝，我快要淹死了

---

1. 西班牙哈莱姆，即美国纽约曼哈顿上城东哈莱姆区西部，初指东哈莱姆区西部，"一战"后大量波多黎各裔人口涌入聚居，故名。

我的生命线 [1] 追随的是不是你

我一直琢磨着关于我的一切

自从我在那里看到你

我驰骋在你野猫般魅力的悬崖上

我知道我在你身旁，但我不知身在何处

你已杀死了我，你已创造了我

我笑得中途掉落了鞋子

我知道了，宝贝，你会伴我左右吗？

那样我就可以辨明我是否真实

---

1. 生命线，亦可解作"救生索"，与上句呼应。

Spanish Harlem Incident

Gypsy gal, the hands of Harlem
Cannot hold you to its heat
Your temperature's too hot for taming
Your flaming feet burn up the street
I am homeless, come and take me
Into reach of your rattling drums
Let me know, babe, about my fortune
Down along my restless palms

Gypsy gal, you got me swallowed
I have fallen far beneath
Your pearly eyes, so fast an' slashing
An' your flashing diamond teeth
The night is pitch black, come an' make my
Pale face fit into place, ah, please!
Let me know, babe, I'm nearly drowning
If it's you my lifelines trace

I been wond'rin' all about me
Ever since I seen you there
On the cliffs of your wildcat charms I'm riding
I know I'm 'round you but I don't know where
You have slayed me, you have made me
I got to laugh halfways off my heels
I got to know, babe, will you surround me?
So I can tell if I'm really real

自由的钟乐

太阳西沉，离午夜断续的鸣钟尚远
我们躲进门道里，雷声轰隆
随着闪电恢宏的钟声敲打着声音中的影子
似乎是自由的钟乐在闪耀
为没有将力量用于战斗的勇士而闪耀
为在手无寸铁的逃亡路上的难民而闪耀
为黑夜里每一名战败的士兵
我们凝视着自由的钟乐在闪耀

在城市的熔炉中，我们藏起脸
意外地望见墙壁在加固
随着婚礼的钟声的回音在雨吹打之前
消融在闪电的钟声里
为反叛者而鸣钟，为浪荡子而鸣钟
为不幸的人、被遗弃和被抛弃的人而鸣钟
为被驱逐的、在危险中持久烧灼的人而鸣钟
我们凝视着自由的钟乐在闪耀

通过狂野扯落的冰雹猛烈而神秘的击打
天空在赤裸裸的奇迹中裂响它的诗篇

萦绕的教堂钟声被远远地吹进微风中

只留下闪电和雷的钟声

为温和的人而敲响，为善良的人而敲响

为心灵的守护者和保护者而敲响

为超越其所属时代的、未受担保的画家

我们凝视着自由的钟乐在闪耀

通过狂野的大教堂之夜，雨水将流言拆散

为没有地位的、被剥夺面目的形象

为那些无处将其思想全然带入

理所当然之境的舌头而鸣钟

为聋人和盲者而鸣钟，为哑巴而鸣钟

为受虐待的人、单身的母亲、被叫错名字的妓女而鸣钟

为受追捕所逐、所欺的轻罪逃犯

我们凝视着自由的钟乐在闪耀

即便云朵的白帘在遥远的角落里闪耀

催眠的泼洒的雾慢慢消散

电灯仍像箭矢一样攻击，射出只为那些

注定要漂泊或被阻止漂泊的人

为那些求索的人而鸣钟，在他们无言的探寻之途上

为内心寂寞的恋人，他们有着过于私密的故事

为每一个无害的、温和的灵魂，他们被错误地投入监狱

我们凝视着自由的钟乐在闪耀

当我回忆起我们被抓获之时，盲目乐观地笑着
被无轨的时辰所困住，因为这些时辰悬而未决
当我们听最后一次，我们看最后一眼
被迷住，被吞没，直到鸣钟结束
为那些疼痛的、创伤无法调治的人而鸣钟
为无数困惑、被控告、被虐待、毒瘾缠身及更糟糕的人
为每一个在整个宽广宇宙中焦虑不安的人
我们凝视着自由的钟乐在闪耀

Chimes of Freedom

Far between sundown's finish an' midnight's broken toll
We ducked inside the doorway, thunder crashing
As majestic bells of bolts struck shadows in the sounds
Seeming to be the chimes of freedom flashing
Flashing for the warriors whose strength is not to fight
Flashing for the refugees on the unarmed road of flight
An' for each an' ev'ry underdog soldier in the night
An' we gazed upon the chimes of freedom flashing

In the city's melted furnace, unexpectedly we watched
With faces hidden while the walls were tightening
As the echo of the wedding bells before the blowin' rain
Dissolved into the bells of the lightning
Tolling for the rebel, tolling for the rake
Tolling for the luckless, the abandoned an' forsaked
Tolling for the outcast, burnin' constantly at stake
An' we gazed upon the chimes of freedom flashing

Through the mad mystic hammering of the wild ripping
  hail
The sky cracked its poems in naked wonder
That the clinging of the church bells blew far into the breeze
Leaving only bells of lightning and its thunder
Striking for the gentle, striking for the kind
Striking for the guardians and protectors of the mind
An' the unpawned painter behind beyond his rightful time
An' we gazed upon the chimes of freedom flashing

Through the wild cathedral evening the rain unraveled tales

For the disrobed faceless forms of no position
Tolling for the tongues with no place to bring their thoughts
All down in taken-for-granted situations
Tolling for the deaf an' blind, tolling for the mute
Tolling for the mistreated, mateless mother, the mistitled
    prostitute
For the misdemeanor outlaw, chased an' cheated by pursuit
An' we gazed upon the chimes of freedom flashing

Even though a cloud's white curtain in a far-off corner flashed
An' the hypnotic splattered mist was slowly lifting
Electric light still struck like arrows, fired but for the ones
Condemned to drift or else be kept from drifting
Tolling for the searching ones, on their speechless, seeking
    trail
For the lonesome-hearted lovers with too personal a tale
An' for each unharmful, gentle soul misplaced inside a jail
An' we gazed upon the chimes of freedom flashing

Starry-eyed an' laughing as I recall when we were caught
Trapped by no track of hours for they hanged suspended
As we listened one last time an' we watched with one last
    look
Spellbound an' swallowed 'til the tolling ended
Tolling for the aching ones whose wounds cannot be nursed
For the countless confused, accused, misused, strung-out
    ones an' worse
An' for every hung-up person in the whole wide universe
An' we gazed upon the chimes of freedom flashing

我将无拘无束十号

我很平庸，也很普通
我就像他，像你一样
我是每个人的兄弟和儿子
我和任何人都没什么不同
和我说话毫无用处
就像和你说话一样

我白天早早地就在打着空拳
我设想自己准备与卡修斯·克莱[1]对击
我说"呸，嘿，咄，哼，卡修斯·克莱，我来了
26，27，28，29，我要让你的脸看起来像我的
五，四，三，二，一，卡修斯·克莱你最好跑掉
99，100，101，102，你妈妈甚至会认不出你
14，15，16，17，18，19，把他打得彻底没脾气"

嗯，我不知道，但我被告知

1.卡修斯·克莱（Cassius Clay，1942—2016），拳王阿里的原名。1964
年2月，阿里甫一出道即大败当时长胜的索尼·利斯顿（Sonny Liston），获
得"重量级拳王"称号。

天堂里的街道镶着黄金

我问你事情如何可以变得更糟

如果俄罗斯人恰好先到了那儿

啊哈！多么可怕！

喏，我是自由派，但在某种程度上

我想要每一个人都自由

但如果你认为我会让巴里·戈德华特[1]

搬到隔壁，娶我的女儿

你肯定认为我疯了！

我不会让他这么做，为了古巴所有的农场

嗯，我把我的猴子放在木头上

命令它做一条狗

它摇摇尾巴，晃晃脑袋

它反倒做出了猫的样子

它是只怪猴子，那么诡异

我坐着，脚上穿着高跟运动鞋

等着在正午的阳光下打网球

---

1. 巴里·戈德华特（Barry Goldwater, 1909—1998），美国政治家，共和党人，有"保守派先生"之称。

我将白色短裤卷过了腰间

我的假发帽落在脸上

但他们不会让我待在网球场上

我有一个女人，她那么卑鄙

她把我的靴子扔进洗衣机

当我裸体时，拿铅弹硌我

把泡泡糖放入我的食物

她很可笑，想要我的钱，就叫我"亲爱的"

喏，我有了一个朋友，他把生命耗费在

用一把猎刀刺穿我的照片

梦想着用一条围巾勒死我

当我的名字出现，他假装呕吐

我有一百万个朋友！

喏，他们要我读一首诗

在女生联谊会之家

我被打倒了，我的脑袋天旋地转

我和女训导胡搅蛮缠

好极了！我是一名诗人，我知道这一点

希望我没有吹嘘

我要让头发长到脚，那么奇怪

所以我看起来像一条行走的山脉

我要骑马来到奥马哈

进入乡村俱乐部和高尔夫球场

携带着《纽约时报》，打入几个洞，让他们震惊

喏，你可能想要知道，到目前为止

这首歌说的是什么

可能让你更加困惑的是

这东西到底有什么用

它什么也不是

这是我在英格兰学到的东西

I Shall Be Free No. 10

I'm just average, common too
I'm just like him, the same as you
I'm everybody's brother and son
I ain't different from anyone
It ain't no use a-talking to me
It's just the same as talking to you

I was shadow-boxing earlier in the day
I figured I was ready for Cassius Clay
I said "Fee, fie, fo, fum, Cassius Clay, here I come
26, 27, 28, 29, I'm gonna make your face look just like
    mine
Five, four, three, two, one, Cassius Clay you'd better run
99, 100, 101, 102, your ma won't even recognize you
14, 15, 16, 17, 18, 19, gonna knock him clean right out of
    his spleen"

Well, I don't know, but I've been told
The streets in heaven are lined with gold
I ask you how things could get much worse
If the Russians happen to get up there first
Wowee! pretty scary!

Now, I'm liberal, but to a degree
I want ev'rybody to be free
But if you think that I'll let Barry Goldwater
Move in next door and marry my daughter
You must think I'm crazy!
I wouldn't let him do it for all the farms in Cuba

Well, I set my monkey on the log
And ordered him to do the Dog
He wagged his tail and shook his head
And he went and did the Cat instead
He's a weird monkey, very funky

I sat with my high-heeled sneakers on
Waiting to play tennis in the noonday sun
I had my white shorts rolled up past my waist
And my wig-hat was falling in my face
But they wouldn't let me on the tennis court

I got a woman, she's so mean
She sticks my boots in the washing machine
Sticks me with buckshot when I'm nude
Puts bubblegum in my food
She's funny, wants my money, calls me "honey"

Now I got a friend who spends his life
Stabbing my picture with a bowie knife
Dreams of strangling me with a scarf
When my name comes up he pretends to barf
I've got a million friends!

Now they asked me to read a poem
At the sorority sisters' home
I got knocked down and my head was swimmin'
I wound up with the Dean of Women
Yippee! I'm a poet, and I know it
Hope I don't blow it

I'm gonna grow my hair down to my feet so strange
So I look like a walking mountain range

And I'm gonna ride into Omaha on a horse
Out to the country club and the golf course
Carry *The New York Times*, shoot a few holes, blow their
minds

Now you're probably wondering by now
Just what this song is all about
What's probably got you baffled more
Is what this thing here is for
It's nothing
It's something I learned over in England

致拉蒙娜

拉蒙娜

靠近点

轻阖你的泪眼

你的悲伤引起的痛苦

会随你神智的恢复而飘逝

城市中的花朵

虽然像在呼吸

有时却像死去一样

试图对付死亡

是徒劳的

尽管我不能以诗行作出解释

你皲裂的土气的嘴唇

我还是想去亲吻

为了要处在你肌肤力量之下

你令人着迷的举动

仍然俘获了我所在的分分秒秒

却使我心伤悲，爱人

看到你努力成为一个

并不存在的世界的一部分

这只是一个梦，宝贝

一场虚空，一个阴谋，宝贝

那将你卷入这样的感觉

我可以看见你的脑袋

已被从嘴里吐出的一文不值的唾沫

所歪曲、喂饱

我看得出，你在

留下还是返回南方之间

左右为难

你被愚弄而以为

终点就在眼前

然而没人要战胜你

没有人要击败你

只是你自感糟糕

我听你说过许多次

你不比谁好

谁也不比你好

如果你真的相信

你知道，你

没有什么可赢取，没有什么可失去

你的悲伤来源于

常来者、权势人物和朋友

炒作你，把你归类

让你感到

你必须和他们一模一样

我会永远和你说话

但很快，我的言辞

会变得毫无意义

因为在我内心深处

我知道我什么忙也帮不上

一切随风而逝

一切变化无常

就做你认为应该做的事

也许有一天

谁知道呢，宝贝

我会出现，在你面前哭泣

To Ramona

Ramona
Come closer
Shut softly your watery eyes
The pangs of your sadness
Shall pass as your senses will rise
The flowers of the city
Though breathlike
Get deathlike at times
And there's no use in tryin'
T' deal with the dyin'
Though I cannot explain that in lines

Your cracked country lips
I still wish to kiss
As to be under the strength of your skin
Your magnetic movements
Still capture the minutes I'm in
But it grieves my heart, love
To see you tryin' to be a part of
A world that just don't exist
It's all just a dream, babe
A vacuum, a scheme, babe
That sucks you into feelin' like this

I can see that your head
Has been twisted and fed
By worthless foam from the mouth
I can tell you are torn
Between stayin' and returnin'

On back to the South
You've been fooled into thinking
That the finishin' end is at hand
Yet there's no one to beat you
No one t' defeat you
'Cept the thoughts of yourself feeling bad

I've heard you say many times
That you're better 'n no one
And no one is better 'n you
If you really believe that
You know you got
Nothing to win and nothing to lose
From fixtures and forces and friends
Your sorrow does stem
That hype you and type you
Making you feel
That you must be exactly like them

I'd forever talk to you
But soon my words
They would turn into a meaningless ring
For deep in my heart
I know there is no help I can bring
Everything passes
Everything changes
Just do what you think you should do
And someday maybe
Who knows, baby
I'll come and be cryin' to you

汽车惊魂[1] 噩梦

我重重敲着一座农舍
想找个地方待下来
我十分，十分疲惫
我来的路很长，很长
我说："嘿，嘿，里面
有没有人在家？"
我站在台阶上
感到极其孤单
好吧，出来一个农民
他一定以为我是疯子
他迅速地看到了我
用枪顶着我的肚子

我跪下了
双膝着地
说："我喜欢农民
别向我开枪，求你了！"
他抬起步枪

---

1. 歌名及歌词内容指涉希区柯克执导的电影《惊魂记》(Psycho，1960)。

并开始大叫

"你是那种旅行推销员

我听说过那样的人"[1]

我说："不！不！不！

我是一个医生，千真万确

我是一个清白的孩子

我也上过大学"

然后他的女儿来了

她的名字叫丽塔

她看起来像是从

《甜蜜的生活》[2]里走出来的

我立即试着让她的爸爸

冷静下来

告诉他，他拥有一座

多么优美、多么漂亮的农场

他说："对于农场

医生都知道些什么，还望相告？"

我说："我出生在

---

1. 英语笑话中常拿旅行推销员背着农夫与其女儿发生关系为笑料。

2. 费里尼于 1960 年执导的电影，出演女主角的安妮塔·艾克伯格（Anita Ekberg）因此走红，成为性感代名词。

一口许愿井的底下"

好吧，看着我指甲里的污垢

我猜他知道我不会撒谎

"我猜你累了"

他有些会意地说道

我说："是的，今天我开车

走了上万英里"

他说："我给你一张床

在炉子下面

只有一个条件

你马上去睡觉

不要碰我的女儿

明天早上，给牛挤奶"

我睡得像一只老鼠

当我听到有东西猛地一动

丽塔站在那里

看起来就像托尼·帕金斯 [1]

她说："你想冲个澡吗？

---

1. 即安东尼·帕金斯（Anthony Perkins，1932—1992），美国演员，在《惊魂记》中扮演具有双重人格的汽车旅馆老板，在浴室中杀死卷款潜逃的女主角。

我可以带你到门口"

我说："哦，不！不！

之前我就去过"

我知道我必须逃离

但我不知道如何做到

当她说

"你想冲澡吗，现在？"

好吧，我不可以离开

除非老人把我赶出去

因为我已经答应了

要给他的牛挤奶

我不得不说些什么

冲撞他，让他感到十分怪异

于是我喊了起来

"我喜欢菲德尔·卡斯特罗和他的胡子"

丽塔看起来受到了冒犯

但她走开了

当他冲下楼梯

说："我听到你说了些什么？"

我说："我喜欢菲德尔·卡斯特罗

我想你听到的是对的"

我缩下头，当他朝我挥舞

用尽全力的拳头

丽塔喃喃自语

说着她在山丘上的母亲

当他的拳头击中冰箱

他说他要杀了我

如果我不在两秒内

走出这扇门

"你这不爱国的

坏烂的医生、反资的叛徒"

嗯，他把一本《读者文摘》

朝我头上扔，我就逃跑了

我翻了个跟头

当我看到他拿起了枪

我破窗而出

以每小时一百英里的速度

轰然坠地

就在他院子的花丛间

丽塔说："回来！"

当他开始装子弹

太阳正在升起

我沿着大路跑去

嗯，我想我不会再回那儿

哪怕一小会

即使丽塔搬走了

在汽车旅馆得到了一份工作

他还在等我

日以继夜，偷偷摸摸

他要把我告发给

联邦调查局

我，我嬉闹，顿足

我在嬉闹时感到庆幸

如果没有言论自由

我可能会身陷泥沼[1]

1.《惊魂记》中凶手杀害女主角后，弃尸泥沼。

Motorpsycho Nightmare

I pounded on a farmhouse
Lookin' for a place to stay
I was mighty, mighty tired
I had come a long, long way
I said, "Hey, hey, in there
Is there anybody home?"
I was standin' on the steps
Feelin' most alone
Well, out comes a farmer
He must have thought that I was nuts
He immediately looked at me
And stuck a gun into my guts

I fell down
To my bended knees
Saying, "I dig farmers
Don't shoot me, please!"
He cocked his rifle
And began to shout
"You're that travelin' salesman
That I have heard about"
I said, "No! No! No!
I'm a doctor and it's true
I'm a clean-cut kid
And I been to college, too"

Then in comes his daughter
Whose name was Rita
She looked like she stepped out of

La Dolce Vita
I immediately tried to cool it
With her dad
And told him what a
Nice, pretty farm he had
He said, "What do doctors
Know about farms, pray tell?"
I said, "I was born
At the bottom of a wishing well"

Well, by the dirt 'neath my nails
I guess he knew I wouldn't lie
"I guess you're tired"
He said, kinda sly
I said, "Yes, ten thousand miles
Today I drove"
He said, "I got a bed for you
Underneath the stove
Just one condition
And you go to sleep right now
That you don't touch my daughter
And in the morning, milk the cow"

I was sleepin' like a rat
When I heard something jerkin'
There stood Rita
Lookin' just like Tony Perkins
She said, "Would you like to take a shower?
I'll show you up to the door"
I said, "Oh, no! no!
I've been through this before"
I knew I had to split
But I didn't know how

When she said
"Would you like to take that shower, now?"

Well, I couldn't leave
Unless the old man chased me out
'Cause I'd already promised
That I'd milk his cows
I had to say something
To strike him very weird
So I yelled out
"I like Fidel Castro and his beard"
Rita looked offended
But she got out of the way
As he came charging down the stairs
Sayin', "What's that I heard you say?"

I said, "I like Fidel Castro
I think you heard me right"
And ducked as he swung
At me with all his might
Rita mumbled something
'Bout her mother on the hill
As his fist hit the icebox
He said he's going to kill me
If I don't get out the door
In two seconds flat
"You unpatriotic
Rotten doctor Commie rat"

Well, he threw a *Reader's Digest*
At my head and I did run
I did a somersault
As I seen him get his gun

And crashed through the window
At a hundred miles an hour
And landed fully blast
In his garden flowers
Rita said, "Come back!"
As he started to load
The sun was comin' up
And I was runnin' down the road

Well, I don't figure I'll be back
There for a spell
Even though Rita moved away
And got a job in a motel
He still waits for me
Constant, on the sly
He wants to turn me in
To the F.B.I.
Me, I romp and stomp
Thankful as I romp
Without freedom of speech
I might be in the swamp

我的往昔岁月

绯红色火焰缠绕于耳畔

翻滚过高处强大的陷阱

被道路上燃烧的火焰所攫住

让意念成为我的地图

"很快，我们会在边缘相遇。"我说

激昂的眉毛下流露着骄傲

啊，但那时我更加苍老

现在我比那时更加年轻

半死不活的偏见向前跳跃

"撕下所有的仇恨。"我尖叫

生活是黑白分明的，这个谎言

从我的头骨中说出。我梦见

火枪手的浪漫之事

变得根深蒂固，不知怎地

啊，但那时我更加苍老

现在我比那时更加年轻

姑娘们的面容构成了前行的道路

从假意嫉妒

到记忆

古老历史的政治

都被僵尸般的布道者抛掉

出乎意外，然而，不知怎地

啊，但那时我更加苍老

现在我比那时更加年轻

自命为教授的舌头

正经得不能开玩笑

喋喋不休地说自由

只是学校里的平等

"平等。"我说出这个词

仿佛说出婚礼誓言

啊，但那时我更加苍老

现在我比那时更加年轻

以士兵的姿势，我用手瞄准

那些教育人的狗杂种

并不惧怕我会成为我的敌人

在我宣讲的时刻

我的道路由骚乱的船指引

从船尾到船头全都叛变

啊，但那时我更加苍老

现在我比那时更加年轻

是的，我的卫士坚忍地守立，当抽象的威胁
高尚得无法忽视
让我误以为
我有些东西需要捍卫
好和坏，我定义这些术语
相当清晰，毫无疑问，不知怎地
啊，但那时我更加苍老
现在我比那时更加年轻

My Back Pages

Crimson flames tied through my ears
Rollin' high and mighty traps
Pounced with fire on flaming roads
Using ideas as my maps
"We'll meet on edges, soon," said I
Proud 'neath heated brow
Ah, but I was so much older then
I'm younger than that now

Half-wracked prejudice leaped forth
"Rip down all hate," I screamed
Lies that life is black and white
Spoke from my skull. I dreamed
Romantic facts of musketeers
Foundationed deep, somehow
Ah, but I was so much older then
I'm younger than that now

Girls' faces formed the forward path
From phony jealousy
To memorizing politics
Of ancient history
Flung down by corpse evangelists
Unthought of, though, somehow
Ah, but I was so much older then
I'm younger than that now

A self-ordained professor's tongue
Too serious to fool

Spouted out that liberty
Is just equality in school
"Equality," I spoke the word
As if a wedding vow
Ah, but I was so much older then
I'm younger than that now

In a soldier's stance, I aimed my hand
At the mongrel dogs who teach
Fearing not that I'd become my enemy
In the instant that I preach
My pathway led by confusion boats
Mutiny from stern to bow
Ah, but I was so much older then
I'm younger than that now

Yes, my guard stood hard when abstract threats
Too noble to neglect
Deceived me into thinking
I had something to protect
Good and bad, I define these terms
Quite clear, no doubt, somehow
Ah, but I was so much older then
I'm younger than that now

不相信你

（她表现得就像我们从未相识）

我无法理解

她放开我的手

把我留在这里对着墙

我真的想要知道

她为什么离去

但我丝毫不能接近她

虽然我们在狂燃之夜亲吻过

她说她永远不会忘记

但此刻早晨明朗

犹如我不在此处

她表现得就像我们从未相识

这一切对我而言是新鲜的

像某种谜

甚至像一个神话

但难以想象

她是昨晚与我

在一起的同一个人

从黑暗中，那些梦被遗弃

我依然在做梦？

我希望她来解答

她的声音再一次说话

而不是表现得就像我们从未相识

倘若她感觉糟糕

那她为什么不告诉我

而是不搭理我呢？

毫无疑问

她似乎走得太远了

我已无法让她回心转意

尽管那个夜晚晕眩旋转

我依然记得她的耳语

但显然她没有

显然她也不会

她表现得就像我们从未相识

如果我不必猜测

我很乐意忏悔

我可能尝试过的任何事情

是否我与她待在一起太久了

或做错了什么

我希望她会告诉我那是什么，我会避开

虽然她的裙子摇曳如吉他弹奏

她的嘴唇水润湿漉

但如今有些事情已经改变

因为她不一样了

她表现得就像我们从未相识

今天我离去

我将会走在自己的路上

对此我说不了太多

但如果你想要我去做

我可以变得和你一样

假装我们从未有过接触

倘若有人问我

"遗忘是否那么容易？"

我会说："轻而易举

你只要选中一个人

然后假装你们从未相识！"

Don't Believe You
(She Acts Like We Never Have Met)

I can't understand
She let go of my hand
An' left me here facing the wall
I'd sure like t' know
Why she did go
But I can't get close t' her at all
Though we kissed through the wild blazing nighttime
She said she would never forget
But now mornin's clear
It's like I ain't here
She just acts like we never have met

It's all new t' me
Like some mystery
It could even be like a myth
Yet it's hard t' think on
That she's the same one
That last night I was with
From darkness, dreams're deserted
Am I still dreamin' yet?
I wish she'd unlock
Her voice once an' talk
'Stead of acting like we never have met

If she ain't feelin' well
Then why don't she tell
'Stead of turnin' her back t' my face?

Without any doubt
She seems too far out
For me t' return t' her chase
Though the night ran swirling an' whirling
I remember her whispering yet
But evidently she don't
An' evidently she won't
She just acts like we never have met

If I didn't have t' guess
I'd gladly confess
T' anything I might've tried
If I was with 'er too long
Or have done something wrong
I wish she'd tell me what it is, I'll run an' hide
Though her skirt it swayed as a guitar played
Her mouth was watery and wet
But now something has changed
For she ain't the same
She just acts like we never have met

I'm leavin' today
I'll be on my way
Of this I can't say very much
But if you want me to
I can be just like you
An' pretend that we never have touched
An' if anybody asks me
"Is it easy to forget?"
I'll say, "It's easily done
You just pick anyone
An' pretend that you never have met!"

朴素 D 调歌谣 [1]

我曾爱上一位姑娘，她有着古铜色的皮肤
天真若羔羊，温雅如小鹿
我骄傲地讨她欢心，可如今她已离去
离去，就像她带走的季节

穿过初夏的微风，我将她偷走
从她母亲和姐姐那里，尽管她们就在近旁
她们个个都被年轻时的挫败所折磨
带着一连串的懊悔，她们努力指引我们

这一对姐妹，我凭借天生的敏感
爱上了妹妹，她是有创造力的那一个
经常当替罪羊，她很容易
被周遭嫉妒的人们毁掉

对她的寄生虫姐姐，我毫无敬意
受缚于她的无聊，捍卫她的骄傲

---

1. 这首歌记记述了 1964 年 3 月迪伦与苏西关系破裂当晚的情景，并谈及与苏西母亲、姐姐的不和。

她反射着他人的无数幻影
作为对她的生活场景和社交的支撑

我自己，对于我所做的一切，我无可辩解
我所经历的变化甚至无法用作
谎言告诉她，希冀着不要失去
这可能是我一生的梦中情人

带着未知的意识，我抓住
一个华丽但心已碎的壁炉台
没有意识到，我已经滑入
爱的虚伪保证之罪

从显现愤怒到强作平静
空洞的应答，声音缺席
直到损毁的墓碑上我读不出问题，但是："求你了
怎么回事，究竟怎么了？"

所以它确实发生了，就像本可被预见的那样
白日梦的永无休止的爆炸
在夜晚的巅峰，国王和王后
让一切都翻滚跌成碎片

"可悲的人！"她的姐姐喊道
"别打扰她，上帝诅咒你，滚出去！"
我身穿盔甲，转过身
把她钉在她卑微的废墟上

一只裸露的灯泡下方，石膏砰砰作响
她姐姐和我在尖叫的战场上
她夹在中间，噪声的受害者
很快便不堪忍受，就像孩子躲在影子里

一切都完了，一切都完了，承认吧，逃走吧
我吐了两次，弯腰，眼泪模糊了我的视线
我的意识已经破碎，我跑入夜晚
将所有爱的灰烬留在身后

风敲打着我的窗户，房间一片潮湿
说我很抱歉的措辞，我仍未找到
我经常想起她，希望她遇到的那个人
能够充分意识到她有多么珍贵

啊，我在监狱里的朋友，他们问我
"多美好，自由的感觉有多美好？"
而我以最神秘莫测的口吻回答
"离开了天空的束缚，鸟儿会自由吗？"

Ballad in Plain D

I once loved a girl, her skin it was bronze
With the innocence of a lamb, she was gentle like a fawn
I courted her proudly but now she is gone
Gone as the season she's taken

Through young summer's breeze, I stole her away
From her mother and sister, though close did they stay
Each one of them suffering from the failures of their day
With strings of guilt they tried hard to guide us

Of the two sisters, I loved the young
With sensitive instincts, she was the creative one
The constant scapegoat, she was easily undone
By the jealousy of others around her

For her parasite sister, I had no respect
Bound by her boredom, her pride to protect
Countless visions of the other she'd reflect
As a crutch for her scenes and her society

Myself, for what I did, I cannot be excused
The changes I was going through can't even be used
For the lies that I told her in hopes not to lose
The could-be dream-lover of my lifetime

With unknown consciousness, I possessed in my grip
A magnificent mantelpiece, though its heart being chipped
Noticing not that I'd already slipped
To a sin of love's false security

From silhouetted anger to manufactured peace
Answers of emptiness, voice vacancies
Till the tombstones of damage read me no questions but,
    "Please
What's wrong and what's exactly the matter?"

And so it did happen like it could have been foreseen
The timeless explosion of fantasy's dream
At the peak of the night, the king and the queen
Tumbled all down into pieces

"The tragic figure!" her sister did shout
"Leave her alone, God damn you, get out!"
And I in my armor, turning about
And nailing her to the ruins of her pettiness

Beneath a bare lightbulb the plaster did pound
Her sister and I in a screaming battleground
And she in between, the victim of sound
Soon shattered as a child 'neath her shadows

All is gone, all is gone, admit it, take flight
I gagged twice, doubled, tears blinding my sight
My mind it was mangled, I ran into the night
Leaving all of love's ashes behind me

The wind knocks my window, the room it is wet
The words to say I'm sorry, I haven't found yet
I think of her often and hope whoever she's met
Will be fully aware of how precious she is

Ah, my friends from the prison, they ask unto me
"How good, how good does it feel to be free?"

And I answer them most mysteriously
"Are birds free from the chains of the skyway?"

那不是我，宝贝

从我的窗前走开
用你自己选定的步调离开
我不是你想要的，宝贝
我不是你需要的
你说你在找一个人
从不懦弱，永远是强者
保护你，保卫你
无论你是对是错
一个为你打开每扇门的人
但那不是我，宝贝
不，不，不，那不是我，宝贝
我不是你要找的那一个，宝贝

从窗台轻轻走开，宝贝
轻轻走在地板上
我不是你想要的，宝贝
我只会让你失望
你说你在找一个人
他将承诺永不分开
一个为你闭上他眼睛的人

一个关闭他心门的人

一个可以为你而死或做更多的人

但那不是我，宝贝

不，不，不，那不是我，宝贝

我不是你要找的那一个，宝贝

回去融入夜色之中，宝贝

里面的一切都是石头做的

这里的一切全都静止

无论如何，我并非孤身一人

你说你在找一个人

你每一次跌倒，他都会将你扶起

不时地为你采撷花朵

每一次都呼之即来

一个终生的伴侣，别无其他

但那不是我，宝贝

不，不，不，那不是我，宝贝

我不是你要找的那一个，宝贝

It Ain't Me, Babe

Go 'way from my window
Leave at your own chosen speed
I'm not the one you want, babe
I'm not the one you need
You say you're lookin' for someone
Never weak but always strong
To protect you an' defend you
Whether you are right or wrong
Someone to open each and every door
But it ain't me, babe
No, no, no, it ain't me, babe
It ain't me you're lookin' for, babe

Go lightly from the ledge, babe
Go lightly on the ground
I'm not the one you want, babe
I will only let you down
You say you're lookin' for someone
Who will promise never to part
Someone to close his eyes for you
Someone to close his heart
Someone who will die for you an' more
But it ain't me, babe
No, no, no, it ain't me, babe
It ain't me you're lookin' for, babe

Go melt back into the night, babe
Everything inside is made of stone
There's nothing in here moving

An' anyway I'm not alone
You say you're looking for someone
Who'll pick you up each time you fall
To gather flowers constantly
An' to come each time you call
A lover for your life an' nothing more
But it ain't me, babe
No, no, no, it ain't me, babe
It ain't me you're lookin' for, babe

丹妮丝

丹妮丝，丹妮丝
姑娘，你在想什么？
丹妮丝，丹妮丝
姑娘，你在想什么？
你闭上双眼
老天知道你不是瞎子

好吧，我可以看见你在笑
但是，哦，你嘴都笑翻了
我可以看见你在笑
但你都笑翻了
好吧，我知道你在大笑
但你在笑什么

好吧，如果你想要将我抛弃
宝贝，我已经被甩掉
如果你想要将我抛弃
宝贝，我已经被甩掉
宝贝，你想要失去我
宝贝，我已经被失掉

好吧，你在做什么

你在飞翔还是跳了起来？

哦，你在做什么

你在飞翔还是跳了起来？

好吧，你喊我的名字

然后说，你刚才舌头打滑

丹妮丝，丹妮丝

你隐于高阁

丹妮丝，丹妮丝

你隐于高阁

我看着你的眼睛深处，宝贝

我只能看见我自己

Denise

Denise, Denise
Gal, what's on your mind?
Denise, Denise
Gal, what's on your mind?
You got your eyes closed
Heaven knows that you ain't blind

Well, I can see you smiling
But oh your mouth is inside out
I can see you smiling
But you're smiling inside out
Well, I know you're laughin'
But what are you laughin' about

Well, if you're tryin' to throw me
Babe, I've already been tossed
If you're tryin' to throw me
Babe, I've already been tossed
Babe, you're tryin' to lose me
Babe, I'm already lost

Well, what are you doing
Are you flying or have you flipped?
Oh, what are you doing
Are you flying or have you flipped?
Well, you call my name
And then say your tongue just slipped

Denise, Denise
You're concealed here on the shelf
Denise, Denise
You're concealed here on the shelf
I'm looking deep in your eyes, babe
And all I can see is myself

如果你要走，现在就走
（不然就留下过夜）

听我说，宝贝

有些事你必须知道

我想和你在一起，姑娘

如果你也想和我在一起

但如果你要走

也没关系

但如果你要走，现在就走

不然就留下过夜

我之所以问你

并不是在做什么测试

只是我没有手表

而你一直在问我几点了

但如果你要走

也没关系

但如果你要走，现在就走

不然就留下过夜

我只是个可怜的家伙，宝贝
指望着与人联系
但我确实不想让你觉得
我得不到什么尊重

但如果你要走
也没关系
但如果你要走，现在就走
不然就留下过夜

你知道我会做噩梦
也会愧疚亏心
如果我妨碍你做什么
你真正想做的事

但如果你要走
也没关系
但如果你要走，现在就走
不然就留下过夜

我并不想要

任何你从未给过的东西
只是我很快要睡了
天太黑，你会找不到门口

但如果你要走
也没关系
但如果你要走，现在就走
不然就留下过夜

If You Gotta Go, Go Now
(Or Else You Got to Stay All Night)

Listen to me, baby
There's something you must see
I want to be with you, gal
If you want to be with me

But if you got to go
It's all right
But if you got to go, go now
Or else you gotta stay all night

It ain't that I'm questionin' you
To take part in any quiz
It's just that I ain't got no watch
An' you keep askin' me what time it is

But if you got to go
It's all right
But if you got to go, go now
Or else you gotta stay all night

I am just a poor boy, baby
Lookin' to connect
But I certainly don't want you thinkin'
That I ain't got any respect

But if you got to go
It's all right

But if you got to go, go now
Or else you gotta stay all night

You know I'd have nightmares
And a guilty conscience, too
If I kept you from anything
That you really wanted to do

But if you got to go
It's all right
But if you got to go, go now
Or else you gotta stay all night

It ain't that I'm wantin'
Anything you never gave before
It's just that I'll be sleepin' soon
It'll be too dark for you to find the door

But if you got to go
It's all right
But if you got to go, go now
Or else you gotta stay all night

妈妈[1]，你一直在我心上

大概是太阳的色彩平直地切去
并且覆盖着我所驻足的十字路口
或许是天气或类似的东西
但妈妈，你萦绕在我心头

我不是故意惹麻烦，请不要贬低我也不要沮丧
我不是在请求也不是在诉说："我难以忘却"
我不会踱步徘徊，卑躬屈膝，可是
妈妈，你一直在我心上

尽管我的脑子糊里糊涂，想法也可能狭隘
你去了何处都不会令我心烦或陷入悲伤
我甚至不在乎你明天在何处醒来
但妈妈，你一直在我心上

我不是要你说"是"或"不是"之类的话
请理解我，我没有地方要让你去往
我只是对着自己呼吸，假装我不知道

---

1. 妈妈，口语中又有"情人""妻子"之意。

妈妈，你一直在我心上

当你在清晨醒来，宝贝，看看镜子里面
你知道我不会在你身旁，你知道我不会在附近
我只是好奇想知道，你能否清晰地看到自己
就像把你放在心上的人那样

Mama, You Been on My Mind

Perhaps it's the color of the sun cut flat
An' cov'rin' the crossroads I'm standing at
Or maybe it's the weather or something like that
But mama, you been on my mind

I don't mean trouble, please don't put me down or get upset
I am not pleadin' or sayin', "I can't forget"
I do not walk the floor bowed down an' bent, but yet
Mama, you been on my mind

Even though my mind is hazy an' my thoughts they might
  be narrow
Where you been don't bother me nor bring me down
  in sorrow
It don't even matter to me where you're wakin' up tomorrow
But mama, you're just on my mind

I am not askin' you to say words like "yes" or "no"
Please understand me, I got no place for you t' go
I'm just breathin' to myself, pretendin' not that I don't know
Mama, you been on my mind

When you wake up in the mornin', baby, look inside your
  mirror
You know I won't be next to you, you know I won't be near
I'd just be curious to know if you can see yourself as clear
As someone who has had you on his mind

花花公子与花花女郎

哦，你们这些花花公子与花花女郎

不会操控我的世界

不会操控我的世界

不会操控我的世界

你们这些花花公子与花花女郎

不会操控我的世界

无论是现在还是其他什么时候

你们这些防核尘地下室的兜售者 [1]

无法进我的家门

无法进我的家门

无法进我的家门

你们这些防核尘地下室的兜售者

无法进我的家门

无论是现在还是其他什么时候

---

1. 在赫鲁晓夫单方面撕毁禁止核试验协议后，美国恢复地下核试验，防核尘
地下室随之销售兴盛，涌现了大量销售人员。

你们这吉姆·克劳[1]之地

无法使我转身离去

无法使我转身离去

无法使我转身离去

你们这吉姆·克劳之地

无法使我转身离去

无论是现在还是其他什么时候

动用私刑的暴民的笑声

不会再发出了

不会再发出了

不会再发出了

动用私刑的暴民的笑声

不会再发出了

无论是现在还是其他什么时候

你们这些谈论战争的疯狂的舌头

不会指引我的道路

不会指引我的道路

---

1. 吉姆·克劳，原为美国喜剧演员托马斯·赖斯（Thomas Dartmouth Rice）创作的黑人舞台角色，表演的歌舞极尽侮辱黑人，却备受当时美国白人的欢迎，后成为歧视黑人的代名词。

不会指引我的道路

你们这些谈论战争的疯狂的舌头

不会指引我的道路

无论是现在还是其他什么时候

你们这些迫害者和种族仇恨分子

不会被绞死在这附近

不会被绞死在这附近

不会被绞死在这附近

你们这些迫害者和种族仇恨分子

不会被绞死在这附近

无论是现在还是其他什么时候

你们这些花花公子与花花女郎

不会拥有我的世界

不会拥有我的世界

不会拥有我的世界

你们这些花花公子与花花女郎

不会拥有我的世界

无论是现在还是其他什么时候

Playboys and Playgirls

Oh, ye playboys and playgirls
Ain't a-gonna run my world
Ain't a-gonna run my world
Ain't a-gonna run my world
Ye playboys and playgirls
Ain't a-gonna run my world
Not now or no other time

You fallout shelter sellers
Can't get in my door
Can't get in my door
Can't get in my door
You fallout shelter sellers
Can't get in my door
Not now or no other time

Your Jim Crow ground
Can't turn me around
Can't turn me around
Can't turn me around
Your Jim Crow ground
Can't turn me around
Not now or no other time

The laughter in the lynch mob
Ain't a-gonna do no more
Ain't a-gonna do no more
Ain't a-gonna do no more
The laughter in the lynch mob

Ain't a-gonna do no more
Not now or no other time

You insane tongues of war talk
Ain't a-gonna guide my road
Ain't a-gonna guide my road
Ain't a-gonna guide my road
You insane tongues of war talk
Ain't a-gonna guide my road
Not now or no other time

You red baiters and race haters
Ain't a-gonna hang around here
Ain't a-gonna hang around here
Ain't a-gonna hang around here
You red baiters and race haters
Ain't a-gonna hang around here
Not now or no other time

Ye playboys and playgirls
Ain't a-gonna own my world
Ain't a-gonna own my world
Ain't a-gonna own my world
Ye playboys and playgirls
Ain't a-gonna own my world
Not now or no other time

ixixxmix I'd talk all nite to you but soon my words would turn into a
                                    meaningless ring
for deep in my heart I know there's no heap I can bring
everything passes. everything changes just do what you think you should do
for someday baby who know maybe I'll come an be cryin t you.

just I add
talk & their time

making you feel like you here & be just like then

全数带回家
Bringing It All Back Home

陈黎 张芬龄 胡续冬　译

发行于 1965 年 6 月 22 日的专辑《全数带回家》，在某种意义上可以看作鲍勃·迪伦音乐风格的转折点。此专辑正反两面的曲风相异，一面延续了之前的风格，以原声木吉他主奏，包括《铃鼓手先生》《伊甸园之门》《没关系，妈（我只不过是在流血）》以及《一切都结束了，蓝宝宝》；另一面进行了创新的探索，迪伦以电音吉他主奏，邀请了摇滚乐队参与录音伴奏。迪伦的创新在当时的民谣圈显得过于离经叛道，一些思想严肃的年轻人尚未意识到将要到来的变革，该专辑在起初招致恶评，但最终还是得到了认可。1979 年的《滚石唱片导览》（Rolling Stone Record Guide）中，美国乐评人戴夫·马尔什（Dave Marsh）给予这张专辑高度的评价："将滚石与披头士乐队中查克·贝里式的节奏，与左派、复兴的民谣传统相结合，迪伦确实将此带回了家，创造出一种新的摇滚乐……可用各种艺术传统形式去摇滚。"

就歌词而言，《铃鼓手先生》《玛吉的农场》等作品运用了许多兰波式的意象、隐喻和通感，具有强烈的超现实主义风格。与前作《在风中飘荡》《暴雨将至》相比，迪伦在该专辑中的语言变得更为个性而抽象，政治倾向亦趋于保守和内省。

专辑封面上有两处耐人寻味的细节：一是迪伦所佩戴的袖扣为琼·贝兹送的礼物，二人关系曾十分亲密，但对音乐和政治的不同看法还是使他们分道扬镳；一是在迪伦身后的红裳女子乃其经纪人之妻莎莉·格罗斯曼（Sally Grossman），她是萨拉·朗兹（Sara Lownds）的朋友，而朗兹后来成为迪伦的第一任妻子。《爱不减／无限》便是献给朗兹的情歌。

本专辑中的《地下乡愁蓝调》《她非我莫属》《玛吉的农场》《爱不减／无限》《铃鼓手先生》及《爱只不过是个脏字》由陈黎先生、张芬龄女士合译，其余数首由胡续冬先生翻译。

编者

地下乡愁蓝调 [1]

约翰尼在地下室

调配着药剂 [2]

我站在人行路

思索着政府

穿着军用风衣的男子

摘掉徽章，歇了工

他说他咳个不停

希望能买药去病

小心啊，小伙子

你捅了个娄子

天知道何时干的事

但你又做了一次

你最好躲进小巷小道

寻找新的同好

戴浣熊皮帽的男子

进了大牢

他要十一块钱

---

1. 歌名源自杰克·凯鲁亚克的小说名字《地下人》（The Subterraneans）。
2. 可能指可待因（Codeine），一种镇咳、镇痛的药品，长期使用有依赖性。

你只弄到十元美钞

玛吉快步走来

脸上满是煤烟

她谈到条子在

被窝里动了手脚

不管怎样电话遭到了窃听

玛吉说消息传不停

他们五月初的搜查已定

地方检察官的命令

小心啊，小伙子

别管你做了何事

踮起脚尖小心翼翼

别吸食兴奋剂

最好少跟那帮老是提着

消防水龙的人混在一起 [1]

要安分守己

当心便衣

你不需要气象员

就该知道吹的是什么风

---

1. 在美国黑人民权运动中，抗议者遭高压消防水枪喷射。

嗑了药人时昏，时飘逸
一心想钻进小穴里去
按门铃去，没把握到底
能不能推销点东西
尽力了，被拒了
回原处，写盲文点字
入狱，弃保逃逸
若不成，就当兵去
小心啊，小伙子
你难逃挨揍一事
但吸毒者、诈骗者
六度的失败者
在戏院四周乱趸
婊子趁乱行事
准备钓新的傻子
别盲从领导
要留意停车计费器

啊，出生，保温
短裤，韵事，学跳舞
穿好衣服，接受祝福
设法当成功人物
取悦她，取悦他，送礼

不偷取，不扒窃

上学二十年

他们排你上日班

小心啊，小伙子

他们隐瞒了所有的事

最好自窨井盖跳入

为自己点根蜡烛

别穿凉鞋

避开丑闻威胁

不想当流浪汉

最好嚼嚼口香糖

泵停摆

因为野蛮人取走了把手[1]

---

1. 以上两行歌词可能指迪伦曾到过的纽约巴德学院，校内有一个无把手的泵。

Subterranean Homesick Blues

Johnny's in the basement
Mixing up the medicine
I'm on the pavement
Thinking about the government
The man in the trench coat
Badge out, laid off
Says he's got a bad cough
Wants to get it paid off
Look out kid
It's somethin' you did
God knows when
But you're doin' it again
You better duck down the alley way
Lookin' for a new friend
The man in the coon-skin cap
In the big pen
Wants eleven dollar bills
You only got ten

Maggie comes fleet foot
Face full of black soot
Talkin' that the heat put
Plants in the bed but
The phone's tapped anyway
Maggie says that many say
They must bust in early May
Orders from the D.A.
Look out kid
Don't matter what you did

Walk on your tiptoes
Don't try "No-Doz"
Better stay away from those
That carry around a fire hose
Keep a clean nose
Watch the plain clothes
You don't need a weatherman
To know which way the wind blows

Get sick, get well
Hang around a ink well
Ring bell, hard to tell
If anything is goin' to sell
Try hard, get barred
Get back, write braille
Get jailed, jump bail
Join the army, if you fail
Look out kid
You're gonna get hit
But users, cheaters
Six-time losers
Hang around the theaters
Girl by the whirlpool
Lookin' for a new fool
Don't follow leaders
Watch the parkin' meters

Ah get born, keep warm
Short pants, romance, learn to dance
Get dressed, get blessed
Try to be a success
Please her, please him, buy gifts
Don't steal, don't lift

Twenty years of schoolin'
And they put you on the day shift
Look out kid
They keep it all hid
Better jump down a manhole
Light yourself a candle
Don't wear sandals
Try to avoid the scandals
Don't wanna be a bum
You better chew gum
The pump don't work
'Cause the vandals took the handles

她非我莫属

她什么都不缺
她是艺术家，不回头看
她什么都不缺
她是艺术家，不回头看
她能让黑暗抽离夜晚
而把白日涂成一片黑暗

刚开始你两脚屹立
自豪为她偷取一切入她眼的东西
刚开始你两脚屹立
自豪为她偷取一切入她眼的东西
到头来却变成自她的钥匙孔偷窥
双膝跪地

她从不摔跤
她无处可跌倒
她从不摔跤
她无处可跌倒
她是没人管的孩子
法律根本动不了她

她戴着一只埃及指环

在她开口之前闪闪发光

她戴着一只埃及指环

在她开口之前闪闪发光

她是催眠有术的收藏家

你是一件会走路的古玩

星期日那天向她俯首称臣

她生日来到向她行礼致敬

星期日那天向她俯首称臣

她生日来到向她行礼致敬

万圣节时送她小喇叭

圣诞节时给她买个鼓

She Belongs to Me

She's got everything she needs
She's an artist, she don't look back
She's got everything she needs
She's an artist, she don't look back
She can take the dark out of the nighttime
And paint the daytime black

You will start out standing
Proud to steal her anything she sees
You will start out standing
Proud to steal her anything she sees
But you will wind up peeking through her keyhole
Down upon your knees

She never stumbles
She's got no place to fall
She never stumbles
She's got no place to fall
She's nobody's child
The Law can't touch her at all

She wears an Egyptian ring
That sparkles before she speaks
She wears an Egyptian ring
That sparkles before she speaks
She's a hypnotist collector
You are a walking antique

Bow down to her on Sunday

Salute her when her birthday comes
Bow down to her on Sunday
Salute her when her birthday comes
For Halloween give her a trumpet
And for Christmas, buy her a drum

玛吉的农场

我不打算再去玛吉的农场干活
是的，我不打算再去玛吉的农场干活
嗯，我早晨醒来
双手交扣，祈求雨降
脑子里塞满一大堆念头
快让我疯狂
她叫我那样擦洗地板真是侮辱我
我不打算再去玛吉的农场干活

我不打算再替玛吉的哥哥干活
是的，我不打算再替玛吉的哥哥干活
嗯，他递给你一枚五美分硬币
他递给你一枚十美分硬币
咧嘴笑着问你
是不是觉得欢喜
然后在你每回大声关门时罚钱强索
我不打算再替玛吉的哥哥干活

我不打算再替玛吉的爸干活
是的，我不打算再替玛吉的爸干活

嗯，他对着你的脸

喷雪茄烟取乐

他卧房的窗

是用砖块砌成的

房门周边有国民警卫队看守

啊，我不打算再替玛吉的爸干活

我不打算再替玛吉的妈干活

是的，我不打算再替玛吉的妈干活

嗯，她对所有的佣人

高谈男人和上帝和法律

大家都说

她是爸背后的主脑

她六十八，却说自己二十四刚过

我不打算再替玛吉的妈干活

我不打算再去玛吉的农场干活

是的，我不打算再去玛吉的农场干活

嗯，我尽全力

想做自己

但大家都希望你

以他们为样例

他们在你做苦工时唱歌，真让我烦透

我不打算再去玛吉的农场干活

Maggie's Farm

I ain't gonna work on Maggie's farm no more
No, I ain't gonna work on Maggie's farm no more
Well, I wake in the morning
Fold my hands and pray for rain
I got a head full of ideas
That are drivin' me insane
It's a shame the way she makes me scrub the floor
I ain't gonna work on Maggie's farm no more

I ain't gonna work for Maggie's brother no more
No, I ain't gonna work for Maggie's brother no more
Well, he hands you a nickel
He hands you a dime
He asks you with a grin
If you're havin' a good time
Then he fines you every time you slam the door
I ain't gonna work for Maggie's brother no more

I ain't gonna work for Maggie's pa no more
No, I ain't gonna work for Maggie's pa no more
Well, he puts his cigar
Out in your face just for kicks
His bedroom window
It is made out of bricks
The National Guard stands around his door
Ah, I ain't gonna work for Maggie's pa no more

I ain't gonna work for Maggie's ma no more
No, I ain't gonna work for Maggie's ma no more

Well, she talks to all the servants
About man and God and law
Everybody says
She's the brains behind pa
She's sixty-eight, but she says she's twenty-four
I ain't gonna work for Maggie's ma no more

I ain't gonna work on Maggie's farm no more
No, I ain't gonna work on Maggie's farm no more
Well, I try my best
To be just like I am
But everybody wants you
To be just like them
They sing while you slave and I just get bored
I ain't gonna work on Maggie's farm no more

爱不减 / 无限 [1]

我的爱人说话不用言语

不带理想或暴力

她不必说自己忠贞不贰

但是她真真实实，像冰，像火

别人拿玫瑰

作出几小时的承诺

我的爱人灿笑如花

情人节礼物无法收买她

在廉价商店和公车站

人们聊着眼下的境况

看书，反复引经据典

在墙上论断一通 [2]

有人高谈未来

我的爱人轻声细语

---

1. 原文直译为爱减零再除以无限。无限，在赌博中指庄家受注无上限，意味着需要承受风险。歌名最初为《廉价商店》，取自第二节第一句歌词"在廉价商店和公车站"。

2.《旧约·但以理书》5:5-28，伯沙撒王的宴会上，"忽有人的指头显出，在王宫与灯台相对的墙上写字"，但以理为王解读文字，说神预告了其国的终结。

192

她知道没有成功能及失败

而失败也绝称不上成功

斗篷和匕首摆荡

女士们点亮烛光

在骑士的仪式上

即便卒子也要心生怼怨

火柴拼成的雕像

接二连三倒塌一地

我的爱人眨眨眼，懒得搭理

她懂得太多不想辩解或评断

桥梁在午夜摇晃

乡村医生闲逛

银行家的外甥女们追求完美

期待智者们带来的所有佳礼

狂风号叫如槌

夜里又湿又冷地吹着

我的爱人像只乌鸦

立在我的窗前，断了单翼

Love Minus Zero/No Limit

My love she speaks like silence
Without ideals or violence
She doesn't have to say she's faithful
Yet she's true, like ice, like fire
People carry roses
Make promises by the hours
My love she laughs like the flowers
Valentines can't buy her

In the dime stores and bus stations
People talk of situations
Read books, repeat quotations
Draw conclusions on the wall
Some speak of the future
My love she speaks softly
She knows there's no success like failure
And that failure's no success at all

The cloak and dagger dangles
Madams light the candles
In ceremonies of the horsemen
Even the pawn must hold a grudge
Statues made of matchsticks
Crumble into one another
My love winks, she does not bother
She knows too much to argue or to judge

The bridge at midnight trembles
The country doctor rambles

Bankers' nieces seek perfection
Expecting all the gifts that wise men bring
The wind howls like a hammer
The night blows cold and rainy
My love she's like some raven
At my window with a broken wing

亡命之徒蓝调

跟跟跄跄地踏进

某个可笑的潟湖是不是很糟糕？

跟跟跄跄地踏进

某个泥泞的潟湖是不是很糟糕？

尤其是在一个零下九度的

下午三点钟

我不会挂上画

我不会挂上画框

我不会挂上画

我不会挂上画框

嗯，我没准看起来像罗伯特·福特

但是我觉得自己像杰西·詹姆斯 [1]

嗯，我希望我在

澳大利亚的山岭上

---

1. 罗伯特·福特（Robert Ford）和杰西·詹姆斯（Jesse James）均为美国 19 世纪恶贯满盈的匪徒。福特本是詹姆斯匪帮中的一员，1882 年为获取赏金，趁詹姆斯挂画时将其枪杀。伍迪·格思里（Woody Guthrie）又有歌曲《杰西·詹姆斯》（Jesse James），形容詹姆斯为无惧战斗与死亡的强梁。

哦，我希望我在

澳大利亚的山岭上

我没任何理由去那儿，但我

想象也许这意味着某种改变

我戴上黑色太阳镜

我留着黑牙为求好运

我戴上黑色太阳镜

我的黑牙带给我好运

一切的一切都别问我

我也许就会告诉你真相

我在杰克逊搞到一个女人

我不会说出她的名字

我在杰克逊搞到一个女人

我不会说出她的名字

她皮肤黝黑，但我

照样爱她 [1]

---

1. 此节歌词可能指涉美国反异族通婚法例，1967 年美国联邦最高法院裁定此
法例违宪而废止。

Outlaw Blues

Ain't it hard to stumble
And land in some funny lagoon?
Ain't it hard to stumble
And land in some muddy lagoon?
Especially when it's nine below zero
And three o'clock in the afternoon

Ain't gonna hang no picture
Ain't gonna hang no picture frame
Ain't gonna hang no picture
Ain't gonna hang no picture frame
Well, I might look like Robert Ford
But I feel just like a Jesse James

Well, I wish I was on some
Australian mountain range
Oh, I wish I was on some
Australian mountain range
I got no reason to be there, but I
Imagine it would be some kind of change

I got my dark sunglasses
I got for good luck my black tooth
I got my dark sunglasses
I'm carryin' for good luck my black tooth
Don't ask me nothin' about nothin'
I just might tell you the truth

I got a woman in Jackson

I ain't gonna say her name
I got a woman in Jackson
I ain't gonna say her name
She's a brown-skin woman, but I
Love her just the same

再次上路

嗯，我早上醒来
袜子里有青蛙
你老妈正藏在
冰柜里边
你老爸戴着拿破仑·波拿巴的面具
走了进来
然后你就问我为什么不住这儿了
亲爱的，你非得问么？

嗯，我去宠宠你的猴子
弄上一脸的抓痕
我问壁炉里的人是谁
你告诉我是圣诞老人
送奶的人来了
戴着顶常礼帽
然后你就问我为什么不住这儿了
亲爱的，你怎么就非得问这个？

嗯，我要了点吃的
我饿得像头猪

于是我吃上了糙米、海带

和一个脏兮兮的热狗

我身上有个无底洞

我的胃在里面无影无踪

然后你就问我为什么不住这儿了

亲爱的，我在想你真是好奇怪

你爷爷的手杖

变成了一把剑

你奶奶对着贴在木板上的

图画祈祷

我口袋里的每一样东西

你叔叔都会偷走

然后你就问我为什么不住这儿了

亲爱的，我不敢相信你是认真的

嗯，厨房里在打架

他们足以把我吓哭

邮差来了

连他都要掺和进来

甚至连管家

都要跑来证明什么

然后你就问我为什么不住这儿了

亲爱的，你为什么还不走？

On the Road Again

Well, I woke up in the morning
There's frogs inside my socks
Your mama, she's a-hidin'
Inside the icebox
Your daddy walks in wearin'
A Napoleon Bonaparte mask
Then you ask why I don't live here
Honey, do you have to ask?

Well, I go to pet your monkey
I get a face full of claws
I ask who's in the fireplace
And you tell me Santa Claus
The milkman comes in
He's wearing a derby hat
Then you ask why I don't live here
Honey, how come you have to ask me that?

Well, I asked for something to eat
I'm hungry as a hog
So I get brown rice, seaweed
And a dirty hot dog
I've got a hole
Where my stomach disappeared
Then you ask why I don't live here
Honey, I gotta think you're really weird

Your grandpa's cane
It turns into a sword

Your grandma prays to pictures
That are pasted on a board
Everything inside my pockets
Your uncle steals
Then you ask why I don't live here
Honey, I can't believe that you're for real

Well, there's fistfights in the kitchen
They're enough to make me cry
The mailman comes in
Even he's gotta take a side
Even the butler
He's got something to prove
Then you ask why I don't live here
Honey, how come you don't move?

鲍勃·迪伦的第 115 个梦

我乘坐着五月花号

我认为我发现了一片陆地

我喊阿拉伯船长 [1]

我让你看个明白

船长跑到甲板上

说："孩子们，别管鲸鱼了

看前边！

关掉引擎

改变航向

拉紧帆索"

我们唱起了那首歌

像所有的糙爷们儿水手

在远航时唱的那样

"我会叫它亚美利加"

我们一踏上陆地我就这么说

---

1. 阿拉伯船长，源自梅尔维尔的小说《白鲸》（Moby-Dick）中的亚哈船长（Captain Ahab），以及美国乡村、流行歌手雷·史蒂文斯（Ray Stevens）的歌曲《阿拉伯的亚哈》（Ahab the Arab）。

我深吸了一口气

跌在地上，险些不能站立

阿拉伯船长开始

起草契约

他说："我们来建一座堡垒

开始用小珠子来买地"

就在这时候一个警察来到街上

完全是个疯子

他把我们都关进了监狱

罪名是携带鱼叉

哦，我逃狱了

别问我怎么做到的

我跑出去求助

我经过一头根西奶牛的身旁

它领着我走到了

包厘街贫民窟

那里的人们扛着标语走来走去

喊着："严禁游手好闲"[1]

我混进了他们的行列

说道："希望我没来迟"

---

1. 严禁游手好闲，谐音"禁止核武器"（ban the bombs）。

这时候我才意识到

我已经连续五天没有吃饭

我跑进一家餐馆

去找厨师

我告诉他们我是

一本著名礼仪书的编辑

英俊的女服务生

他[1] 穿着浅灰蓝色的披风

我点了叙泽特[2]，我说

"麻烦你做那种可丽饼"

这时候整个厨房

被沸腾的油脂引爆

食物到处乱飞

我帽子都没拿就离开了

现在，我不想再管闲事了

但我走进了一家银行

去给阿拉伯船长和牢房里

所有的弟兄们弄点保释金

---

1. 原文如此。
2. 叙泽特，一种倒烈酒燃烧的可丽饼。

他们问我要抵押品

我脱下我的裤子

他们就把我扔到了巷里

这时候走来一个法国姑娘

她邀请我去她家里

我去了，但是她有个朋友

他把我砸晕

抢走了我的靴子

又把我扔回了街头

好吧，我敲了敲一户人家的门

他家还飘着美国国旗

我说："你能帮帮忙吗?

我的朋友们遇上点麻烦"

那人说："滚开

我要把你大卸八块"

我说："你知道，他们也拒绝过耶稣"

他说："你才不是耶稣

在我打断你骨头之前快滚开

我又不是你爹"

我决定让人逮捕这家伙

我跑去找警察

我跑了出来

跳进了一辆出租车

从另一扇门出去 [1]

一个英国人说："好极了" [2]

他看着我跳过一个热狗摊

和一辆停在

楼对面的马车

那座楼宣扬弟兄情谊

我径直跑进前门

像一个流浪水手一样

但那里只是一座殡仪馆

那人盘问了我是谁

我又说了一遍我的朋友们

都在监狱里，他叹了口气

递给我一张名片

他说："他们死了就给我打电话"

我握了握他的手说再见

我跑到街上

---

1. 以上两行歌词指涉"披头士狂热"时期，披头士曾以车队作阻隔，从车的
一侧开门穿过来躲避歌迷。
2. 指涉披头士的昵称"Fab Four"。

一个保龄球一路滚过来

撞到了我的脚

一个收费电话响了起来

我莫名兴奋起来

接起电话应答着喂

一只脚越过了线

好了，到这会儿

我已经烦透了

试着给我的朋友们和阿拉伯船长

带去任何帮助

我决定抛一枚硬币

让正反面

来指引我到底是该

回到船上还是回到监狱

于是我抵押了我的水手服

换来一枚硬币抛了起来

硬币抛出了反面

反和帆押韵 [1]

所以我决定回到船上

---

1. 硬币的反面（tail）和船帆（sail）互韵，其实亦与监狱（jail）相押。

好吧，我回来了，取下了

桅杆上违章停泊的罚单

我正把它撕成碎片

海岸警卫队的船开了过来

他们问我叫什么名字

我说："基德船长 [1]"

他们信了我，但是

他们想知道

我到底做了些什么

我说我受雇于

乌鲁克的教皇 [2]

他们立即就放我走了

他们怕得要死

嗯，最后我听说阿拉伯船长

迷上了一头鲸鱼 [3]

那鲸鱼已经嫁给了监狱的

副警长

但最搞笑的事情是

---

1. 基德船长，即威廉·基德（William Kidd，1654—1701），苏格兰水手，因海盗罪被处决。

2. 乌鲁克的教皇，迪伦杜撰的一个人物。Eruke，中古英语解作"蠕虫"。

3. 鲸鱼，俚语有"肥婆"之意，且呼应亚哈船长追捕白鲸的执着。

当我离开海湾的时候

我看见三艘船鼓满风帆[1]

齐刷刷向我驶来

我问船长叫什么名字

为什么他没开卡车

他说他叫哥伦布

我只好说："祝你走运"

---

1. 哥伦布在 1492 年第一次远航的船队，乃由三艘帆船组成。

Bob Dylan's 115th Dream

I was riding on the Mayflower
When I thought I spied some land
I yelled for Captain Arab
I have yuh understand
Who came running to the deck
Said, "Boys, forget the whale
Look on over yonder
Cut the engines
Change the sail
Haul on the bowline"
We sang that melody
Like all tough sailors do
When they are far away at sea

"I think I'll call it America"
I said as we hit land
I took a deep breath
I fell down, I could not stand
Captain Arab he started
Writing up some deeds
He said, "Let's set up a fort
And start buying the place with beads"
Just then this cop comes down the street
Crazy as a loon
He throw us all in jail
For carryin' harpoons

Ah me I busted out
Don't even ask me how

I went to get some help
I walked by a Guernsey cow
Who directed me down
To the Bowery slums
Where people carried signs around
Saying, "Ban the bums"
I jumped right into line
Sayin', "I hope that I'm not late"
When I realized I hadn't eaten
For five days straight

I went into a restaurant
Lookin' for the cook
I told them I was the editor
Of a famous etiquette book
The waitress he was handsome
He wore a powder blue cape
I ordered some suzette, I said
"Could you please make that crepe"
Just then the whole kitchen exploded
From boilin' fat
Food was flying everywhere
And I left without my hat

Now, I didn't mean to be nosy
But I went into a bank
To get some bail for Arab
And all the boys back in the tank
They asked me for some collateral
And I pulled down my pants
They threw me in the alley
When up comes this girl from France
Who invited me to her house

I went, but she had a friend
Who knocked me out
And robbed my boots
And I was on the street again

Well, I rapped upon a house
With the U.S. flag upon display
I said, "Could you help me out
I got some friends down the way"
The man says, "Get out of here
I'll tear you limb from limb"
I said, "You know they refused Jesus, too"
He said, "You're not Him
Get out of here before I break your bones
I ain't your pop"
I decided to have him arrested
And I went looking for a cop

I ran right outside
And I hopped inside a cab
I went out the other door
This Englishman said, "Fab"
As he saw me leap a hot dog stand
And a chariot that stood
Parked across from a building
Advertising brotherhood
I ran right through the front door
Like a hobo sailor does
But it was just a funeral parlor
And the man asked me who I was

I repeated that my friends
Were all in jail, with a sigh

He gave me his card
He said, "Call me if they die"
I shook his hand and said goodbye
Ran out to the street
When a bowling ball came down the road
And knocked me off my feet
A pay phone was ringing
It just about blew my mind
When I picked it up and said hello
This foot came through the line

Well, by this time I was fed up
At tryin' to make a stab
At bringin' back any help
For my friends and Captain Arab
I decided to flip a coin
Like either heads or tails
Would let me know if I should go
Back to ship or back to jail
So I hocked my sailor suit
And I got a coin to flip
It came up tails
It rhymed with sails
So I made it back to the ship

Well, I got back and took
The parkin' ticket off the mast
I was ripping it to shreds
When this coastguard boat went past
They asked me my name
And I said, "Captain Kidd"
They believed me but
They wanted to know

What exactly that I did
I said for the Pope of Eruke
I was employed
They let me go right away
They were very paranoid

Well, the last I heard of Arab
He was stuck on a whale
That was married to the deputy
Sheriff of the jail
But the funniest thing was
When I was leavin' the bay
I saw three ships a-sailin'
They were all heading my way
I asked the captain what his name was
And how come he didn't drive a truck
He said his name was Columbus
I just said, "Good luck"

铃鼓手先生 [1]

嘿！铃鼓手先生，为我奏一曲
我还不困，也不打算上哪儿去
嘿！铃鼓手先生，为我奏一曲
在叮当作响的早晨，我将随你而去

虽然我知道黄昏的帝国已然回归黄沙
自我手中消逝
留我茫然伫立于此却仍无睡意
我的疲倦让我惊异，我双脚烙了印
没有要见的人
空荡荡的老街一片死寂，无梦可寻

嘿！铃鼓手先生，为我奏一曲
我还不困，也不打算上哪儿去
嘿！铃鼓手先生，为我奏一曲
在叮当作响的早晨，我将随你而去

---

1. 歌曲灵感源自 1964 年 2 月，迪伦和几个朋友在公路旅行途中的新奥尔良
看到的狂欢节景象。"铃鼓手先生"的原型是与迪伦合作、善击手鼓的吉他手
布鲁斯·兰霍恩（Bruce Langhorne），也令人联想到德国民间传说中诱走小
孩的花衣笛手。

带我搭乘你的回旋魔船与你同游

我的感官已被剥夺，双手无法握紧

脚趾麻木寸步难行

只有等待皮靴后跟拖我四处流浪

我准备到任何地方，准备隐入

我的单人游行队伍，对我施展你飞舞跃动的魔力

我甘心为其醉迷

嘿！铃鼓手先生，为我奏一曲

我还不困，也不打算上哪儿去

嘿！铃鼓手先生，为我奏一曲

在叮当作响的早晨，我将随你而去

你或许听见笑声，急旋，狂荡，越过艳阳

那并不针对谁而发，只是一路奔逃

而除了天空，再无任何栅栏阻挡

你若依稀听见轻巧旋跃的韵律

与你的铃鼓应和，那只是一名衣衫褴褛尾随在后的小丑

我对此毫不在意

他追逐的只是你眼中的一个影子

嘿！铃鼓手先生，为我奏一曲

我还不困，也不打算上哪儿去

嘿！铃鼓手先生，为我奏一曲
在叮当作响的早晨，我将随你而去

就带着我消失吧，穿过我意识的烟圈
沉入雾蒙蒙的时间废墟，越过冻僵的寒叶
阴森可怖的树林，去到起风的海滩
远离狂悲摧折之境
是的，在钻石天空下起舞，单手自由地挥摆
让大海为我剪影，让马戏团的沙子环抱我
将所有的回忆和命运逐入海浪深处
让我忘掉今天，在明天到临之前

嘿！铃鼓手先生，为我奏一曲
我还不困，也不打算上哪儿去
嘿！铃鼓手先生，为我奏一曲
在叮当作响的早晨，我将随你而去

Mr. Tambourine Man

Hey! Mr. Tambourine Man, play a song for me
I'm not sleepy and there is no place I'm going to
Hey! Mr. Tambourine Man, play a song for me
In the jingle jangle morning I'll come followin' you

Though I know that evenin's empire has returned into sand
Vanished from my hand
Left me blindly here to stand but still not sleeping
My weariness amazes me, I'm branded on my feet
I have no one to meet
And the ancient empty street's too dead for dreaming

Hey! Mr. Tambourine Man, play a song for me
I'm not sleepy and there is no place I'm going to
Hey! Mr. Tambourine Man, play a song for me
In the jingle jangle morning I'll come followin' you

Take me on a trip upon your magic swirlin' ship
My senses have been stripped, my hands can't feel to grip
My toes too numb to step
Wait only for my boot heels to be wanderin'
I'm ready to go anywhere, I'm ready for to fade
Into my own parade, cast your dancing spell my way
I promise to go under it

Hey! Mr. Tambourine Man, play a song for me
I'm not sleepy and there is no place I'm going to
Hey! Mr. Tambourine Man, play a song for me
In the jingle jangle morning I'll come followin' you

Though you might hear laughin', spinnin', swingin' madly
   across the sun
It's not aimed at anyone, it's just escapin' on the run
And but for the sky there are no fences facin'
And if you hear vague traces of skippin' reels of rhyme
To your tambourine in time, it's just a ragged clown behind
I wouldn't pay it any mind
It's just a shadow you're seein' that he's chasing

Hey! Mr. Tambourine Man, play a song for me
I'm not sleepy and there is no place I'm going to
Hey! Mr. Tambourine Man, play a song for me
In the jingle jangle morning I'll come followin' you

Then take me disappearin' through the smoke rings of
   my mind
Down the foggy ruins of time, far past the frozen leaves
The haunted, frightened trees, out to the windy beach
Far from the twisted reach of crazy sorrow
Yes, to dance beneath the diamond sky with one hand
   waving free
Silhouetted by the sea, circled by the circus sands
With all memory and fate driven deep beneath the waves
Let me forget about today until tomorrow

Hey! Mr. Tambourine Man, play a song for me
I'm not sleepy and there is no place I'm going to
Hey! Mr. Tambourine Man, play a song for me
In the jingle jangle morning I'll come followin' you

伊甸园之门

真理在战争与和平中扭曲

其宵禁的鸥鸟滑翔

牛仔天使骑在

四条腿的森林云朵上

他的蜡烛被点燃成太阳

阳光被涂上了黑蜡

除了当它在伊甸园的树下

街灯柱袖手站立

它的铁爪紧贴在

婴儿号哭的洞穴下的路边

虽然它荫蔽着金属徽章

归根到底它只会倒塌

发出轰然而毫无意义的巨响

伊甸园之门从未传出声音

蛮族的战士将头颅插进沙土中

而后抱怨起

没有穿鞋的猎人,他耳已聋

但依然

在海滩上，猎狗朝着船只吠叫

那些船挂着印花的帆

驶往伊甸园之门

拿着时间锈蚀的指南针叶片

阿拉丁和他的神灯

和乌托邦的隐修僧们一起

侧坐在金牛犊[1]上

在他们对天堂的允诺中

你不会听见笑声

除了在伊甸园之门里面

他们在翅膀下低声说起

所有制的所有关系

让那些有罪的人照此行事

并等待继任的王者们

我试图和落寞的麻雀唱出的歌

融为一体

伊甸园之门里面没有王者

---

1. 金牛犊，《旧约·出埃及记》中摩西在西奈山领受"十诫"时以色列人崇拜的偶像，后引申为"假神"之意。

黑色圣母像摩托

双轮吉普赛女王

她那镶银的幽灵

让灰色法兰绒的侏儒尖叫

他对着邪恶的猛禽哭泣

它们了解他那些面包屑一样的罪恶

伊甸园之门里面没有罪恶

经验的王国

在珍爱的风中朽败

乞丐们交换起财物

每个人都想要别人的东西

公主和王子

争论着什么是真实的什么不是

伊甸园之门里面这都无所谓

异国的太阳斜视着

一张从不属于我的床

朋友们和其他的陌生人

试图退出他们的宿命

让人可以完全彻底自由地

去做除死亡之外任何想做的事

伊甸园之门里面没有审判

黎明时分我的爱人来到我身边

向我讲述她的梦

她并没打算把惊鸿一瞥

都铲进每个人意指的沟渠

有时候我觉得除了它们

没有任何词语可以传达真理

而伊甸园之门外面没有真理

Gates of Eden

Of war and peace the truth just twists
Its curfew gull just glides
Upon four-legged forest clouds
The cowboy angel rides
With his candle lit into the sun
Though its glow is waxed in black
All except when 'neath the trees of Eden

The lamppost stands with folded arms
Its iron claws attached
To curbs 'neath holes where babies wail
Though it shadows metal badge
All and all can only fall
With a crashing but meaningless blow
No sound ever comes from the Gates of Eden

The savage soldier sticks his head in sand
And then complains
Unto the shoeless hunter who's gone deaf
But still remains
Upon the beach where hound dogs bay
At ships with tattooed sails
Heading for the Gates of Eden

With a time-rusted compass blade
Aladdin and his lamp
Sits with Utopian hermit monks
Sidesaddle on the Golden Calf
And on their promises of paradise

You will not hear a laugh
All except inside the Gates of Eden

Relationships of ownership
They whisper in the wings
To those condemned to act accordingly
And wait for succeeding kings
And I try to harmonize with songs
The lonesome sparrow sings
There are no kings inside the Gates of Eden

The motorcycle black madonna
Two-wheeled gypsy queen
And her silver-studded phantom cause
The gray flannel dwarf to scream
As he weeps to wicked birds of prey
Who pick up on his bread crumb sins
And there are no sins inside the Gates of Eden

The kingdoms of Experience
In the precious wind they rot
While paupers change possessions
Each one wishing for what the other has got
And the princess and the prince
Discuss what's real and what is not
It doesn't matter inside the Gates of Eden

The foreign sun, it squints upon
A bed that is never mine
As friends and other strangers
From their fates try to resign
Leaving men wholly, totally free
To do anything they wish to do but die

And there are no trials inside the Gates of Eden

At dawn my lover comes to me
And tells me of her dreams
With no attempts to shovel the glimpse
Into the ditch of what each one means
At times I think there are no words
But these to tell what's true
And there are no truths outside the Gates of Eden

没关系，妈
（我只不过是在流血）

午间休憩时分的黑暗[1]

甚至在银匙上都投下了阴影

连带手工制作的刀锋，儿童的气球

同时蚀去了太阳和月亮

要清楚你知道得太早

所有的尝试都毫无意义

尖锐的威胁，轻蔑地发出恐吓

自杀的言谈撕裂自

愚人金号嘴，那空洞号角

演奏着废话，证明了这样一句警言：

人不是忙于出生就是忙于去死

诱惑的役童夺门而出

你跟随他，发现自己置身于战争中

目睹怜悯的瀑布咆哮着溅落

---

1. 可能指英籍匈牙利裔作家阿瑟·库斯勒（Arthur Koestler）的小说名字《正午的黑暗》（*Darkness at Noon*）。

你想要呻吟，但与从前不同的是
你发现自己不过是
又一个哭泣的人

因此当你听到一个陌生的声音
钻进你的耳朵，请不要害怕
没关系，妈，我只不过是在叹息

有人告捷，有人倒台
那些叫嚷着
"让所有该死的人都在地上爬"的人
眼中自有或大或小的道理
而另一些人则说不要仇恨任何事物
除了仇恨本身

觉醒的词语像子弹嗒嗒地响
人类的诸神为满足他们的目标
创造出一切事物，从闪光的玩具枪
到在黑暗中发光的肉色基督
不用望多远就可以轻易地看到
没多少东西真的是神圣的

牧师们在宣讲罪行的下场

教师们在讲授知识时刻准备着
它们通向装着百元大钞的盘子
美德藏身于它的门后
但即使是美利坚合众国的总统
有时候也不得不裸身站立

虽然一路上的规则都已内定
但你所要逃避的只是人类的游戏
没关系，妈，我能做到

广告牌在欺骗你
让你以为你是那个
能做从未做过的事情的人
能赢从未赢过的局面的人
与此同时外面的生活
一如既往地包围着你

你迷失自我，你再度出现
你突然发现自己已经无所畏惧
你独自站立，远离他人
当一个模糊而颤抖的遥远声音
惊醒了你沉睡的耳朵，你听见
有人觉得他们的确找到了你

你神经里的疑惑已被点燃

尽管你知道仍没有合适的答案

来说服你，确保你不会放弃

将它存留在心中，不要忘记：

你不属于

他或者她或者他们或者它

虽然大师们为智慧人和愚昧人

都制订了规则

但我无以为基准，妈

那些必定服从威权的人

他们对威权其实一点也不尊重

那些鄙视他们的工作、他们的命途的人

嫉妒地谈论起悠闲的他们

他们把花种养成

地地道道的投资品

一些人遵照原则甘受

严格党纲束缚的洗礼

社会俱乐部男扮女装、遮遮掩掩

局外人可以自由地批评

然而他们只知道说出要崇拜谁

而后说一句让上帝保佑他

一个用火中之舌[1]唱歌的人
在彼此较劲的合唱队中咕咕噜噜
他在社会的铁钳中扭曲变形
在意的不是往上爬得更高
而是往下把你拖入
他所置身的洞穴中

但我无意伤害或指责
任何一个生活在地穴中的人
但没关系，妈，如果我不能让他开心

老太太法官们注视着成双成对的人
限制性行为，她们敢于
推行假道德，瞪眼辱骂
而金钱从不说话，它诅咒着[2]
淫秽，谁会真正在意
宣传，一切都是欺骗

1.《新约·使徒行传》2:3-4，圣灵化作如火的舌头分赐门徒，他们便得到了口才。
2. 金钱从不说话，反用谚语"金钱万能"（money talks）。诅咒，此处也有"赌咒""发誓"之意。

他们为不曾见过的事物辩护

带着杀手的自豪和安全感

极度无情地打击着心智

对那些认为死亡的真诚

不会自然而然地光顾他们的人

生命有时候必须是一场孤寂

我的眼睛迎面撞向密密麻麻的

墓地和伪神，我拖着脚行走在

野蛮粗暴的琐碎之上

在桎梏里颠来倒去地行走

我踢着腿想要挣脱

好吧，我已经受够了

还有什么新鲜把戏？

如果我那些思想之梦可以被看见

它们很可能会把我的脑袋放上断头台

但没关系，妈，这就是生活，只不过是生活

It's Alright, Ma
(I'm Only Bleeding)

Darkness at the break of noon
Shadows even the silver spoon
The handmade blade, the child's balloon
Eclipses both the sun and moon
To understand you know too soon
There is no sense in trying

Pointed threats, they bluff with scorn
Suicide remarks are torn
From the fool's gold mouthpiece the hollow horn
Plays wasted words, proves to warn
That he not busy being born is busy dying

Temptation's page flies out the door
You follow, find yourself at war
Watch waterfalls of pity roar
You feel to moan but unlike before
You discover that you'd just be one more
Person crying

So don't fear if you hear
A foreign sound to your ear
It's alright, Ma, I'm only sighing

As some warn victory, some downfall
Private reasons great or small
Can be seen in the eyes of those that call

To make all that should be killed to crawl
While others say don't hate nothing at all
Except hatred

Disillusioned words like bullets bark
As human gods aim for their mark
Make everything from toy guns that spark
To flesh-colored Christs that glow in the dark
It's easy to see without looking too far
That not much is really sacred

While preachers preach of evil fates
Teachers teach that knowledge waits
Can lead to hundred-dollar plates
Goodness hides behind its gates
But even the president of the United States
Sometimes must have to stand naked

An' though the rules of the road have been lodged
It's only people's games that you got to dodge
And it's alright, Ma, I can make it

Advertising signs they con
You into thinking you're the one
That can do what's never been done
That can win what's never been won
Meantime life outside goes on
All around you

You lose yourself, you reappear
You suddenly find you got nothing to fear
Alone you stand with nobody near
When a trembling distant voice, unclear

Startles your sleeping ears to hear
That somebody thinks they really found you

A question in your nerves is lit
Yet you know there is no answer fit
To satisfy, insure you not to quit
To keep it in your mind and not forget
That it is not he or she or them or it
That you belong to

Although the masters make the rules
For the wise men and the fools
I got nothing, Ma, to live up to

For them that must obey authority
That they do not respect in any degree
Who despise their jobs, their destinies
Speak jealously of them that are free
Cultivate their flowers to be
Nothing more than something they invest in

While some on principles baptized
To strict party platform ties
Social clubs in drag disguise
Outsiders they can freely criticize
Tell nothing except who to idolize
And then say God bless him

While one who sings with his tongue on fire
Gargles in the rat race choir
Bent out of shape from society's pliers
Cares not to come up any higher
But rather get you down in the hole

That he's in

But I mean no harm nor put fault
On anyone that lives in a vault
But it's alright, Ma, if I can't please him

Old lady judges watch people in pairs
Limited in sex, they dare
To push fake morals, insult and stare
While money doesn't talk, it swears
Obscenity, who really cares
Propaganda, all is phony

While them that defend what they cannot see
With a killer's pride, security
It blows the minds most bitterly
For them that think death's honesty
Won't fall upon them naturally
Life sometimes must get lonely

My eyes collide head-on with stuffed
Graveyards, false gods, I scuff
At pettiness which plays so rough
Walk upside-down inside handcuffs
Kick my legs to crash it off
Say okay, I have had enough
What else can you show me?

And if my thought-dreams could be seen
They'd probably put my head in a guillotine
But it's alright, Ma, it's life, and life only

一切都结束了，蓝宝宝

现在你必须离开了，带走你需要的东西，你认为够用了
但无论你想留下什么，你最好都快点拿走
你的弃子拿着枪站在那边
哭得像太阳中的火焰
当心，圣徒们快走过来了
一切都结束了，蓝宝宝

高速公路是属于赌徒的，你最好多想想
把你碰巧收集到的都带走吧
你的街区里那个两手空空的画师
正在你的床单上绘制疯狂的图案
这片天空也在你身下折叠起来
一切都结束了，蓝宝宝

你的所有晕船的水手都成群结队开船回家
你的所有驯鹿军队都朝着家乡进发
刚刚走出你家门口的恋人
已经从地板上拿走了他所有的毛毯
就连地毯，也在你身下移动
一切都结束了，蓝宝宝

把垫脚石留在身后吧，某种事物在召唤你

忘掉你已经辞别的死者，他们不会再跟随你

正在敲你房门的流浪汉

穿着你以前穿过的衣服

擦亮另一根火柴吧，重新开始

一切都结束了，蓝宝宝

It's All Over Now, Baby Blue

You must leave now, take what you need, you think will last
But whatever you wish to keep, you better grab it fast
Yonder stands your orphan with his gun
Crying like a fire in the sun
Look out the saints are comin' through
And it's all over now, Baby Blue

The highway is for gamblers, better use your sense
Take what you have gathered from coincidence
The empty-handed painter from your streets
Is drawing crazy patterns on your sheets
This sky, too, is folding under you
And it's all over now, Baby Blue

All your seasick sailors, they are rowing home
All your reindeer armies, are all going home
The lover who just walked out your door
Has taken all his blankets from the floor
The carpet, too, is moving under you
And it's all over now, Baby Blue

Leave your stepping stones behind, something calls for you
Forget the dead you've left, they will not follow you
The vagabond who's rapping at your door
Is standing in the clothes that you once wore
Strike another match, go start anew
And it's all over now, Baby Blue

加利福尼亚

（《亡命之徒蓝调》早期版本）

我要去南方

去边境线那边

我要去南方

去边境线那边

一个肥胖的大妈

一度亲过我的嘴

嗯，今天早上我就得走

一丝犹豫也没有

我的行李箱已经收拾好了

我的衣服已经出去晃悠了

旧金山很棒

你肯定能晒够太阳

旧金山很棒

你肯定能晒够太阳

但我习惯于四季分明

加利福尼亚只有一季可浪

嗯，我戴上黑色太阳镜

我留着黑牙为求好运

我戴上黑色太阳镜

为求好运我留着黑牙

一切的一切都别问我

我也许就会告诉你真相

California
(Early version of "Outlaw Blues")

I'm goin' down south
'Neath the borderline
I'm goin' down south
'Neath the borderline
Some fat momma
Kissed my mouth one time

Well, I needed it this morning
Without a shadow of doubt
My suitcase is packed
My clothes are hangin' out

San Francisco's fine
You sure get lots of sun
San Francisco is fine
You sure get lots of sun
But I'm used to four seasons
California's got but one

Well, I got my dark sunglasses
I got for good luck my black tooth
I got my dark sunglasses
And for good luck I got my black tooth
Don't ask me nothin' about nothin'
I just might tell you the truth

别了，安吉丽娜

别了，安吉丽娜

王冠上的铃铛

已被匪徒盗走

我必须追随那声音

三角铁丁零作响

小号缓慢吹奏

别了，安吉丽娜

天空在燃烧

我必须走了

没必要生气

没必要责备

没什么要证明

一切都如常

只是有一张桌子

空空地立在海边

别了，安吉丽娜

天空在颤抖

我必须离开

扑克里的侍从和皇后

抛弃了这个院子

五十二个吉普赛人

现在排队经过门卫

在那里二点的纸牌

和 A 纸牌曾一度失控

别了，安吉丽娜

天空在折叠

不久之后我会再见到你

看，斗鸡眼的海盗们

安坐栖居在太阳里

他们用短管霰弹枪

射击锡罐

每次射中

邻居们都鼓掌欢呼

别了，安吉丽娜

天空变了颜色

我得快点离开

金刚和一群小精灵

在屋顶上跳着

瓦伦蒂诺式的探戈 [1]

而化妆者的手

替死者合上了眼睛

不让任何人感到尴尬

别了，安吉丽娜

天空让人难为情

我必须闪了

机关枪在咆哮

傀儡们投掷石块

魔鬼们把定时炸弹

固定在时钟的指针上

随你怎么称呼我

我绝不会不认

别了，安吉丽娜

天空在爆发

我必须去安静的地方

Farewell Angelina

Farewell Angelina
The bells of the crown
Are being stolen by bandits
I must follow the sound
The triangle tingles
And the trumpets play slow
Farewell Angelina
The sky is on fire
And I must go

There's no need for anger
There's no need for blame
There's nothing to prove
Ev'rything's still the same
Just a table standing empty
By the edge of the sea
Farewell Angelina
The sky is trembling
And I must leave

The jacks and the queens
Have forsaked the courtyard
Fifty-two gypsies
Now file past the guards
In the space where the deuce
And the ace once ran wild
Farewell Angelina
The sky is folding
I'll see you in a while

See the cross-eyed pirates sitting
Perched in the sun
Shooting tin cans
With a sawed-off shotgun
And the neighbors they clap
And they cheer with each blast
Farewell Angelina
The sky's changing color
And I must leave fast

King Kong, little elves
On the rooftops they dance
Valentino-type tangos
While the makeup man's hands
Shut the eyes of the dead
Not to embarrass anyone
Farewell Angelina
The sky is embarrassed
And I must be gone

The machine guns are roaring
The puppets heave rocks
The fiends nail time bombs
To the hands of the clocks
Call me any name you like
I will never deny it
Farewell Angelina
The sky is erupting
I must go where it's quiet

爱只不过是个脏字

仿佛就在昨天
我把思虑抛诸脑后
在吉普赛咖啡店
和朋友的朋友
她坐着，婴孩重重压在膝上
却高谈不受奴役的生活
眼里不见半丝愁影闪过
我听到最早与她有关的一个说辞：
爱只不过是个脏字

在临街一扇不规则的窗户外面
猫咪喵喵叫到天亮
我，也闭上了嘴
对你我无言以对
我的经验有限而且没什么料
我躲着，当你开口说话
对着你孩子的爸
你或许以为我没有，但我确然闻之
你说爱只不过是个脏字

我悄悄地道别

朝自己游戏中的事物推进

漂进漂出于无以

名之的诸般人生

寻找我的替身，寻找

彻底蒸发之道

虽然尝试得其门而入但未奏效

我当时一定以为再没有比这

更荒谬的了：爱只不过是个脏字

虽然我未曾弄懂你的意思

当你对你的男人说话时

我只能从自己的角度思考

而今我明白了

在一次次醒来思索后我看到

那理当永存的圣吻

在烟雾中破灭，那宿命

袭向陌生人身上，恣意而行

是的，我懂了，是我自设陷阱

我不必真的

相信爱只不过是个脏字

Love Is Just a Four Letter Word

Seems like only yesterday
I left my mind behind
Down in the Gypsy Café
With a friend of a friend of mine
She sat with a baby heavy on her knee
Yet spoke of life most free from slavery
With eyes that showed no trace of misery
A phrase in connection first with she I heard
That love is just a four letter word

Outside a rambling storefront window
Cats meowed to the break of day
Me, I kept my mouth shut, too
To you I had no words to say
My experience was limited and underfed
You were talking while I hid
To the one who was the father of your kid
You probably didn't think I did, but I heard
You say that love is just a four letter word

I said goodbye unnoticed
Pushed towards things in my own games
Drifting in and out of lifetimes
Unmentionable by name
Searching for my double, looking for
Complete evaporation to the core
Though I tried and failed at finding any door
I must have thought that there was nothing more
Absurd than that love is just a four letter word

Though I never knew just what you meant
When you were speaking to your man
I can only think in terms of me
And now I understand
After waking enough times to think I see
The Holy Kiss that's supposed to last eternity
Blow up in smoke, its destiny
Falls on strangers, travels free
Yes, I know now, traps are only set by me
And I do not really need to be
Assured that love is just a four letter word